D0883585

As If After Sex

Also by Joseph Torchia

The Kryptonite Kid

As If After Sex

A novel by

Joseph Torchia

A William Abrahams Book
Holt, Rinehart and Winston
New York

Copyright © 1983 by Joseph Torchia
All rights reserved, including the right to reproduce
this book or portions thereof in any form.
First published in February 1984 by Holt, Rinehart
and Winston, 383 Madison Avenue, New York,
New York 10017.
Published simultaneously in Canada by Holt, Rinehart
and Winston of Canada, Limited.

Library of Congress Cataloging in Publication Data
Torchia, Joseph.
As if after sex.
"A William Abrahams book."
I. Title.
PS3570.067A9 1984 813'.54 83-8497
ISBN 0-03-062858-X

First Edition

Design by Lucy Albanese
Printed in the United States of America
10 9 8 7 6 5 4 3 2 1

ISBN 0-03-062858-X

For my brother Butch. And for Brooks, my other. And with special appreciation to—and of—Nell . . .

And to the memory of Moon, who orbits us still . . .

. . . We poets cannot walk the way of beauty without Eros as our companion and guide. We may be heroic after our fashion, disciplined warriors of our craft, yet we are like women, for we exult in passion, and love is still our desire—our craving and our shame.

—Plato, *Dialogues*

As If After Sex

Julian was so hard. He pumped his muscles and puffed up his veins as if he were sculpting himself. He stood in front of mirrors that captured parts of other mirrors that surrounded him with himself. He could flex and stretch himself spectacularly into place, seeing both front and rear at once, making sure every square inch fit perfectly into perspective. He had an image of himself that he had to maintain—and which was constantly reinforced by the refracted stares of other men who moved inside his mirrors. The room was black and silver, leather and steel, metal and glass and music pumped everywhere at once. Julian moved through it like the oxygen moving through his veins. He would strap himself into one machine after another, working first his thighs, then his calves, then his chest or arms or neck. Each machine had its job. Each exercise was designed specifically for a certain part of his body. The slower he pressed against the enormous weights the more he could feel the pain pressing back on him, actually *into* him—and into the shape of what he was yet to be. In order to build up, he must first tear down. That was the most important rule of body building. He would never work the same muscle two days in a row. He would allow a day for the muscle to rest and repair itself—build itself up bigger and stronger, so there would be more to tear down the next time. He imagined his body as layer after layer of scar tissue, torn down and built up through a gradual process of pain and perfect control. He was in harmony when he hurt. He had his shape in his hands, and the eyes in the mirrors were watching.

The equipment, Julian knew, was called Nautilus. It was named after the chambered nautilus, that cephalopod mollusk found in the South Pacific and Indian oceans which builds itself a unique shell—a series of hard, pearly chambers that it inhabits one at a time, each in its turn, for the expanse of its life. Julian had no trouble appreciating the significance of this trademark. He looked at the large blue shell painted on the far wall—it was several feet taller than the machinery which surrounded it—and imagined it as *his* symbol. The container of his life. It was embossed on his membership card and carried in the wallets of all these muscled men who moved amid reflections. Whenever Julian presented it at the door in exchange for towel and locker key, he actually thought of himself as being admitted inside the caverns of some exotic shell. And whenever he strapped himself against the leather seat and steel frame of the chest machine—where he could look up at that painted blue shell as he pressed on the massive weights—he would immediately take a deep breath and try to imagine what a mollusk looked like. Then he would send his arms rising, his chest heaving, his heart pounding, his sweat pouring, his grunts screaming out pain and exhaustion as his blood pumped furiously to supply the oxygen his muscles needed to complete their task—to push harder and higher, up and actually out of that monstrous shell on the wall above him, as if he were the rare and wonderful creature which inhabited it.

It was more than a game Julian played with himself—it was his way of looking at himself. And it was the way the others were now looking at him—at him, not at his image in glass. He was by no means the biggest or most muscular man in the room, but he was by far the hardest, the firmest, the most determined to contain the pain which shaped him. One look at his body heaving and sweating, crying and hurting, and there was no turning back to the mirrors. Those powerful men were powerless against his hard skin, his dark sounds, his flushed face, his fierce determination—and their own desire to have what they could not be. His pain seemed to speak to them. They understood implicitly, with every wet surge of his rippling response to those weights, that whatever they could see before them, and whatever they might eventually be able to touch, would never give them what Julian was giving himself. He was building from within. He was making himself complete, almost Godlike in the way he could create himself, and yet he was so perfectly and utterly man.

That one word seemed to explain what those men wanted, and wanted to be. I watched them watching Julian. I watched for months, long before I ever met Julian—before I actually spoke to him. Even the men with bloated arms and powerful legs and virile tangles of dark hair exploding across massive chests seemed like women in their craving for him. It was not only the way they watched Julian hurting and struggling with those incredible weights—and with himself. It was what happened after he let go of those weights and returned to his feet, his body taut, his muscles suddenly splashing into tiny spasms of relief as the sweat poured down him, actually spewed out of him—curling his blond hair and caressing his smooth skin and making him sparkle. Actually glow. As if the light were not being reflected on him, but issuing *from* him. Inhabiting even his eyes. Looking back at those men with new defiance—new definitions—forcing them to retreat with eyes to the mirrors as he made his way to the locker room, his white shorts saturated with sweat, those eyes clinging like cloth to the promise of what lay hidden. And I saw it all.

I do not exclude or exempt myself.

I admit I am one of those men who followed Julian to the lockers.

I do not pretend I did not watch him peeling off those wet shorts again and again, day after day. I memorized his schedule.

I made sure he would never be there without me.

At night I sometimes dreamed about him. On my way to the gym I would often rehearse in my mind what I would say if ever I got the chance to speak to him.

Even now, as I sit here writing about him—and waiting for him to appear at my doorstep—all I can see is elastic expanding and Julian standing there naked and awesome. His shorts in his hand. Too perfect to approach even with words.

And yet approach him I did—on a humid spring evening when the gym was crowded and the windows were open and Julian was oozing spectacularly onto the floor. Every machine was occupied, every reflection was frantic. Even the moon outside was rising and multiplying itself in mirrors. It was as if that full moon were pulling on Julian's blood, pumping it ever harder and fuller, threatening to explode his veins and send that hard metal crashing through the shell on the wall, and everybody was watching him. Everybody was *imitating* him. I'd never seen a night so heavy and wet with thrust. Even the music was louder than usual. And it wasn't classical or folk, as it often was during the day. Instead it was a punk-rock group screaming "Whip it! Whip it *good*!" And then it was the Rolling Stones singing "You can't always get what you want . . ."

And I couldn't help being swept away by it, carried into it. Not just imitating Julian, but joining him. Mounting the machine right next to him and strapping myself in and adjusting the weights to the furthest limits of my stamina, looking up at that shell on the wall and then looking over at Julian and knowing instinctively that we were of the same species. Of course I didn't put it into those words—it wasn't until much later that

Julian told me what that shell on the wall meant to him. But I translated it instantly into feeling—a sensation that shook me, overtook me, sent my arms pressing and my breath heaving and my muscles screaming at Julian. Actually talking to him through my pores. Telling him in no uncertain terms that I was there with him, wanting him, wanting him to look back at me. And yet knowing my wanting was part of the pain—caught up in the refrain of pumps and grunts that grew and finally drew all eyes onto me and Julian. Me *with* Julian. As if we were bound together by the same furious commotion. As if we were locked in a display of surges and thrusts which swept me away, making me pump beyond all previous expectations, causing my blood to boil, my breath to bloat and finally burst as I collapsed helplessly back into myself, back into that machine, far away from Julian—feeling suddenly naked and afraid. And abandoned, as if after sex.

How else do I explain it? How else do I tell you what happened in that one furious moment of my imagination? How else do I describe the impact it had on everything that was to come? Even before I met Julian he was changing my life. I quickly realized those muscled men were now looking at *me*, watching me untangle myself from that towering machine and taking my first steps into what seemed like a new shape. I could see it staring back. It was as if their eyes were mirrors. And yet it wasn't until I turned and confronted myself in the real mirrors that I saw how truly terrible and transformed I was. My shoulders were hunched and my arms were swollen; and my eyes were ablaze; and my entire body was heaving and oozing, threatening to spring forward like some wounded animal. I jumped back as if to escape myself. I saw panic. I saw fear. I can still see it now. I can still remember the pain of Julian's reflection walking away from me, disappearing toward the stairs as if nothing had ever happened. I can still see the horror of literally hundreds of open eyes and heavy arms and full moons suddenly ricocheting from every corner of the room, reflected in reflections, reaching out and caging me in my enormous image—that savage shape which instinctively pulled back and reared up and made me want *out* of there; away from those men; down those stairs and out that door and into the night—and into a mirror—with Julian.

It happened so fast.

I didn't even bother to shower.

I wore my dark odor like a suit of armor as I stepped out on the streets and lit a cigarette and waited for Julian in the shadows.

And knew what I would do.

No matter what it cost me, no matter where he took me.

I didn't try to define it. Or to blame it on the full moon. Or even to excuse it by saying I'm a writer in search of material.

It was much darker than that.

It was much deeper than anything I could ever explain or contain on paper.

Even as I sit here trying, I laugh at myself. I sip my coffee. I reach for another cigarette. I realize that to look back is to confront self with self, as if in a mirror—to see things so exactly the same that they are completely different.

I do not pretend it is otherwise.

And yet you should have seen the way Julian suddenly exploded out of there, his hair still wet, his jacket slung over his shoulder, his thighs and buttocks threatening to burst through faded jeans.

It was as if he were still naked—or *more* than naked.

Everything he hid with his clothes he accentuated with his clothes. Everybody noticed it.

Every eye on the street was immediately on him, watching him, watching me step out of the shadows to follow him—looking at me contemptuously for being so blatant about my secret desire.

Even the women turned around.

Even the men with women somehow managed to look without looking.

But Julian ignored them all—and me.

He never once gave any indication that he knew I was following him.

Even as he made his way down bright boulevards and past posh shops and among flashing headlights he never turned around.

He kept moving faster and faster, as if he were late for an appointment.

And yet I never suspected anything. I was too caught up in my own deliberate emotion. I didn't realize until too late that his motion was carrying me beyond bright lights, away from frantic intersections, into a world that was darker and dirtier and much more deliberate than anything I could have imagined.

I remember at one corner three men were laughing, joking, drinking canned beer from paper bags and spitting hot smoke into the humid night. They were talking about a stabbing that had occurred in that same spot three weeks ago.

At another corner a woman with long, black legs and a short, white skirt leaned against a building and winked her eye as Julian passed by. She watched him disappearing into shadows, reappearing under neon, finally dissolving into darkness—into a maze of liquor stores and bars, adult bookstores and porno movie houses and cheap hotels with wheezing walls, snickering halls, double locks on the door, maybe a view of an alley.

She deliberately winked at me, too.

She deliberately reminded me of every awful article I had ever read—or written—about this part of town.

Why just a month earlier a waitress was shot in broad daylight—during the breakfast rush—by a man who refused to pay for his eggs-over-easy and hash browns.

And just down this same street a man was discovered dead in a garbage can, minus his balls, by a bag lady searching for scraps one morning. According to police it was another "link" in the chain of very bizarre homosexual murders that had been sweeping the city. One report I read said investigators believed the murderer was homosexual himself—a man who could not "cope with his reality." They also believed he was blond, about six-one, and he doodled on napkins at bars. Witnesses reported they saw such a man leaving a neighborhood bar with another man who was later discovered in a dark alley—minus his clothes and his tongue. That had been just two weeks earlier.

Why was I remembering it now?

What the hell did any of this mean?

The longer I followed Julian the more I thought he was leading me into a dark dream. And yet everything was so stark—so excruciatingly *real.* The garbage and the shadows and an old man lying in a puddle of his own piss. It was as if Julian were purposely taking me as far as possible from the antiseptic smell and fluorescent lights of the locker room. It was as if he were guiding me—telling me those fluorescent lights allowed no shadows, revealed too much. I somehow felt he wanted me to feel alone, afraid, completely out of touch—imagining myself as a statistic or a headline. Or a shadow—not a man. I can see that now.

I can say that now.

His mystery seemed to multiply with each step he took. The landscape was lurid, foreign—lurking with strange shapes and hidden meanings. Even the jacket Julian carried over his shoulder seemed to be part of a deformed shape that twisted its way in front of me—a hunchback or a madman or a werewolf being transformed by the long shadows of the moon. My imagination went wild.

A chill shot through me.

My lungs heaved and my heart pounded and yet my feet had no choice but to head forward, go onward, race inward—shooting ahead as I leaped back in my mind, trying to find something to hold on to. A dream. A memory. Some fragment of a lost image. A sandy beach or a sunny day or a flat expanse of Florida ocean—anything to take me out of here. Away from now.

Back to what I used to be.

How it happened is how it always happens. I push a button and I'm pressing keys in my mind. I'm going back and further back in order to surge ahead. I'm trying not to tantalize you toward that eventual confrontation with Julian—but to take you there. Make you inhabit every step that led me to it and eventually through it, as if I'm examining chambers that have long been abandoned. As if I'm seeing shapes I can never again fit into.

You must bear with me.

You must realize time is not always what it appears to be.

Every line I write takes me further into the future and deeper into the past.

Every day I know that Julian has been here and gone—stepping between paragraphs.

I'm not just pressing on keys—I'm pressing on bruises.

Every time I return to these words they hurt and swell me into perspective. They make me see I have always been alone.

And yet I was glad to be alone that day I first arrived here from Florida. It was as if I were arriving in a new frame of mind—not just a new place. I took a bus from the airport to the heart of the city and I smiled openly at everybody. I had quit my job and I had sold my car and I had saved some money and I was on my own. Nobody knew me here. I could define myself here. I could say who I am and know it was true here. No longer would I carry other people's shape around with me, as if it were some heavy shell that weighted me down to their "reality." I was not going to crawl slowly upon their ground. Instead I was rearing up, leaping out and soaring spectacularly to the other side of the continent. I didn't even want to drive. Or take a bus or train. That was too slow. That would give me time to make a transition in my mind. I just wanted to be dropped here like a bomb and left to explode wide open on my own. All at once. From the air. Into a world that would see and know and respond to my combustion. Feel it back. Explode on their own—from whatever Florida they came from.

I stepped down from that bus and my toes touched the concrete like spark plugs. I looked at everybody as a potential combustion. I clutched my suitcase and walked to the curb and held my breath and knew it was the last day of the year. I had planned it that way. I had decided to start my new life with a new year—and to keep a careful account of it. I purposely bought a blank notebook in Florida and carried it with me onto the plane, making my first entry somewhere over Colorado. It said, simply, "This notebook is me. I am beginning . . ." and I knew those words were with me now. Not just in my mind as I followed Julian, but under my arm as I took my first steps into the city. A real *city*.

A place that seemed to climb up and turn in on itself.

No room for palm-lined boulevards.

No space for long perspectives or perfectly landscaped lives.

Here everything came at me quickly, fiercely—as if the concrete itself were alive—and I had to respond to it.

I had no choice but to look back at those tall buildings as if they were scales on some monstrous body—as if the hovering fog were breath. Even the manhole covers and subway entrances and revolving glass doors all seemed to lead inward, as if through pores, toward a heart. Never had I felt anything pounding so furiously—or carrying me away so completely. Everywhere I looked people and cars went hurrying over it, scurrying into it—down windswept streets, around sharp corners, between big and ever-bigger buildings—hurling past me or crashing into me and saying "Excuse me."

Or: "Come back to Jesus!"

Or: "Got a quarter?"

Or: "Happy New Year!"

"Happy New Year!"

"Happy New Year!"

The first time I heard it I thought those words were speaking directly to me—to *my* new beginning.

But then a window suddenly opened from above and another man shouted "Happy New Year!" as he dumped a boxful of ticker tape and calendar pages from a fifth-floor window.

And then another window opened—and another, and another—from the fourth floor, from the second floor, from the eighth floor—and before I knew it people were standing at office windows everywhere, with drinks and paper in their hands, laughing and waving and toasting and tossing the old year away.

Instantly the world was transformed.

Calendar pages swirled like snowflakes from the clouds. Computer readouts surged like snowdrifts between big buildings, beneath cars, around curbs, through revolving glass doors. Even the ticker tape seemed to hang like icicles from window ledges, stoplights, phone booths, awnings, shrubs, shoppers—and me!

I couldn't help being carried away by it—swept into it. People were not only hurling past me—but hurling the past *at* me. One woman dumped an entire wastebasket. Another woman shouted "Good riddance!" as she tossed her desk calendar to the wind. The higher the buildings got, the deeper it seemed to surround me. Suddenly I found myself skip-roping down those streets with my suitcase, plucking pages out of midair with my free hand as if I were reaching back in time—or reaching ahead to Julian—trying to find out something about my own life. About my *new* life.

Sept. 27: "Take car in tomorrow."

Oct. 8: "Salary advance."

March 21: "Caroline's birthday."

Sept. 15: "Father's deathday."

Aug. 12: "Do payroll."

April 17: "VD Clinic today."

June 1: "Send check for mother's nursing home."

Dec. 31: "Hiii. My name's Michelle. I work on the sixth floor of Macy's. If you're young, hot, handsome, and have no plans for New Year's eve, why don't you stop by the bedding department? We're open tonight till 6."

Instantly I exploded into laughter.

I couldn't help myself.

I could hear it echoing in doorways.

I thought it so funny—that my first proposition should come from a piece of paper. And from a woman.

And from the wind.

It hit me with all the absurdity of a pie in my face.

I dropped my suitcase and threw up my arms and started waving at windows—just for the hell of it. Just in case Michelle might be watching.

But just then a cab pulled over to the curb. A window rolled down.

I tried to tell the driver it was a mistake but I was laughing too hard.

He wanted to know what was so funny.

I told him something was happening here that could happen no other place in the world.

He said, "You must be a tourist."

I said, "Hell no, I moved here—I belong here!"

He said, "Well where are you going?"

I said, "Through the past—into the future!"

He said, "Don't get smart with me, buddy—do you want a cab or don't you?"

But then he smiled.

He looked me right in the eyes as if he knew me. Or somebody like me.

"Well, c'mon," he finally said. Then paused. Then winked. Then said very seriously:

"If it's the future you want, step into my time machine."

How could I resist *that*?

It was more than the tone of his voice or the twinkle in his eye—it was the unrealness of the entire situation. It was the way everything seemed to speak to me—first the city and then a storm and now a smile. One right after another—on top of each other—as if in a dream.

Or a reflection.

See what I mean? Nothing stands still. Not even the past. Not even this page. When I slow things down I distort them. They lose the true motion that makes them alive. The rest is frozen images—a reproduction—memory mounted on a machine.

Words pressed into a blank notebook.

I know all that.

I knew it the moment I tossed Michelle's note over my shoulder, back to the wind.

She was not the only woman I had left behind.

Or was it *woman* I had left behind?

What led me into that cab is what had led me out of Florida. It was all the same thing. It was all part of the same deliberate motion—and emotion. Of course I didn't understand it as logically or as systematically as I present it to you now (or even as clearly as I followed it after Julian that night); but I knew, somehow, as soon as he turned on the windshield wipers to brush away the past, that this cab driver—this mustached man with magical eyes and a mysterious voice—was about to deliver me across new boundaries in a machine that suddenly seemed not so much a place, but a state of grace.

To an apartment I had arranged through an ad.

He wanted to know where I was from.

I said Florida.

He wanted to know what it's like there.

I said everybody's old, even the young people.

He wanted to know what I did for a living.

I said I was a reporter—sometimes a writer.

He wanted to know if I had a job lined up.

I said not yet. I said I wanted time for myself.

"Time?" he said, then slammed on his brakes as a flurry of calendar pages suddenly swept across his windshield. "Well let me tell you, buddy—there's a lot of time here. And there's a lot of self here, too."

He chuckled as if he knew something I didn't.

He shifted down into first gear.

He wanted to know if I was married.

I told him he was awfully talkative.

He told me that words were action.

I told him the truth—that women demanded too much. That it was their nature to hold on. That I wanted to have my own shape.

He thought that was the funniest thing he had ever heard.

He nearly ran over a man with a briefcase.

He wanted to know what "nature" meant.

I told him it was a noun.

I told him it came from the Latin verb *nasci*—and from its past participle *natus*, which means "to be born."

I told him it meant essence, disposition, temperament, or character. That it was the creative and controlling force in the universe. That it was also an inner force or the sum of such forces in an individual. That it was also a spontaneous attitude, as of generosity. I even went so far as to say it might very likely be the external world in its entirety—man's original or natural condition, or a simplified mode of life resembling this condition—and then I told him it appeared on the same page of Webster's dictionary as the word *nautilus.*

I could see his mouth hanging open in the rearview mirror.

I could see a crazy look—a wild look in his eyes, as if he recognized something in me.

He stopped at a light and wanted to know if I was a pansy.

That was the word he used—"pansy."

And yet there was no way I could take offense. Even his voice seemed to smile.

"This city's full of pansies," he laughed as the light turned green. "Wait till you see them under a full moon. You do know what a pansy is, don't you?"

He shifted and speeded up a hill.

The "snow" was getting sparse.

"Yes," I said matter-of-factly. "Yes, it comes from the French *pensée.* It means, literally, 'thought.' "

But he didn't hear me.

At that moment a woman stepped off a curb and he honked and swerved to avoid her.

"I see it every day," he was saying. "I pick a lot of them up the way I picked you up. They flock here as if it's a garden and they sprout entire neighborhoods and then they can't get out. It's kind of sad, in a way. For a lot of them there's no other place they can grow. You're not one of them, are you?"

"Of them?" I said. "What do you mean—*of* them?"

"The pansies," he said. "The queers. The sissies. The homos. The *gays,*" he laughed, as if he thought that was the funniest of all. "The possessed and the dispossessed—at least until they come here.

"This is the one place they're *not* queer," he said.

"Don't you see? When they get here they have to put their sexuality into perspective. They have to confront themselves as people. They have to see who they are—and how much it has to do with where they were.

"They are *were*wolves, in a sense," he laughed and shifted smoothly into third. "Or even better, fraternity brothers. You belonged to a fraternity in college, didn't you? I was in TKE. Pronounced 'teak,' like the wood. Very butch, very macho. Anyway, you run into a guy years later who was in the same fraternity—it doesn't even have to be the same college, or even the same state—and right away you know something about him. You can talk about beer blasts and sorority girls and pledge nights and homecoming floats and how it used to be.

"Well it's just like that—only it used to be awful. So awful that they didn't even wear fraternity pins. So awful that they don't even recognize each other until they come here. And then they recognize each other all too well.

"They have gone through the same initiation.

"They are brothers in the most basic sense.

"They try to make up for lost time.

"They circle back, they spiral forward through streets.

"They hunt and sniff out the past.

"They howl at the full moon.

"I see it all the time," he said as a final flurry of paper swept across our field of vision. "Not just in the back of my cab, but in the apartment next door. The grocery on the corner. Some of the cab drivers I work with. Even my dentist.

"It's the weirdest thing to see so many men living and moving among men.

"They're like palindromes," he said, and his voice was getting excited. And his hands were motioning at the windshield. And we were climbing higher and higher—up a hill, between rows of Victorian houses, away from the crowded downtown area.

And then he said, "You know what a palindrome is, don't you?"

And I said, "Sure, but I don't get the connection."

And he said, "Well give me an example."

And so I said, "Eve is a sieve."

And so he said, "Madam, I'm Adam."

And so I said, "Pull up if I pull up."

And so he laughed and said, "A man, a plan, a canal—Panama."

And so I said, "Lewd did I live, evil I did dwel."

And so he said, "No evil shahs live on."

And so I said, "Did I . . . Did I see bees? I did . . . I did!"

And suddenly we both exploded into furious giggles and recognized something in each other.

Something that suddenly made perfect sense.

And then he said, "I was always good in English. Even majored in it for a while. Even fancied myself as a writer at one time. Thought someday I'd write a conversation—maybe even a poem—entirely in palindromes. But then I switched over to liberal arts. And then to industrial arts. I was a lot better at working with my hands than I was with my head.

"But I always loved to read," he said. "And I always loved palindromes. Especially when they're just one word—like *deified*. No matter which way you look at it, it's still the same direction. Backward to forward, forward to backward, letter for letter—it's still *deified*. Everything's turned inward, everything's reflected outward—just like the pansies.

"Just like a mirror.

"They all converge as they emerge out of themselves.

"Let me put it this way," he said. "You make a palindromic sentence and what have you got? A collection of letters that form words that make the same sense—and the same sentence—whether you read it forward or backward. That's simple enough.

"But when you read it backward there are subtle differences. In order to be true you must rearrange the spaces. In order to give proper emphasis you must change the punctuation and capitalization.

"Well that's the way it is here. Men press against men in a desperate search for subtle differences. They try to compress each other's spaces, punctuate each other's lives. The whole thing's so damned contrived. They make their sameness—their *homo*-ness—so shit-faced important that they end up turning themselves away from the rest of the world.

"It just ain't real," he said. "It takes too much energy—too much manipulation. I found that out when I was trying to compose my poem."

His voice had lost its giggle.

He was getting more serious now.

He was driving toward a point.

The hills were getting higher.

"Let me give you a better example," he said. "An example from life, not language. You see, one night I picked up this guy in front of a bar on Market Street and he was drunk. Really drunk. Threw up on the side of my cab before he even got in. I knew there was a full moon and at first I thought he was gay but then I wasn't quite sure. Normally I wouldn't even pick up such a guy but I felt kind of sorry for him. I mean he wasn't badly dressed and he couldn't have been more than thirty and he had this really pathetic look in his eyes and I guess I'm a sucker for losers. Anyway right away he starts talking about how everybody's like a big piece of Swiss cheese only everybody's got his holes in different places. Only he isn't slurring his words or slobbering all over himself like you'd expect. In fact it's just the opposite. He's so drunk that he's perfectly lucid, almost eloquent, like a professor delivering a lecture. Or a preacher giving a very slow sermon. Except all he can talk about is Swiss cheese. About how people need another piece of cheese to make them complete. About how some people meet other people and when they're together they are whole because their holes are in different places. Because together they are a solid block of cheese with No. Holes. Showing.

"Honest to God, that's just the way he talked. I could see each word going separately through the air, right over the front seat, like smoke rings.

"Except suddenly he stops talking and starts crying and then he's leaning over the front seat and looking up at the moon and whispering in my ear how some people never manage to meet the right piece of cheese. How some people always manage to have a hole showing no matter who they meet or where they go. These people are holy, he whispers.

"They're mystics, he whispers.

"Sometimes they're even prophets, he whispers.

"Usually they're perverts, he whispers.

"And let me tell you I was nervous as hell. I mean one moment he was crying and then he was whispering and then he was laughing and howling and hysterically telling me about *his* holes—about how he takes his sins and puts them in all his holes. About how he orders a drink and pours that in. About how he looks at the moon and shoves that in. About how he flags down a cab or buys a dildo or cuts his hair or clips his nails or masturbates in front of mirrors and stuffs it all in his holes. 'I fill myself up with myself and with pornography!' he says. 'I'm complete in myself!' he says.

"But then the really scary thing happens. Suddenly he shifts to one side of the cab and looks out the window. And when I turn a corner he shifts to the other side. And then to the backside, as if he thinks somebody is following us. And then he turns to me and says very deeply, very deliberately, in a voice which contains its own eerie echo: 'I can't sleep when there's a full moon. I just can't. I've got to watch it so it doesn't hurt somebody.'

"Man was I glad when we finally got to the address he had given me—which turns out to be another bar in a dark alley in an even seedier area of town. Instantly he jumps out of my cab and stands at my window and stares up at the moon for a full minute before he reaches into his pocket and pulls out a twisted wad of bills.

"Only he doesn't look at it as he hands it to me.

"He won't take his eyes off the sky.

"He keeps nervously shifting around.

"His eyes have a wild look, a crazy look.

"He doesn't realize he's also handing me a crumpled bar napkin with doodles all over it.

"I don't realize it either until he has already disappeared into shadows.

"And then I count the bills and find the napkin and see a piece of Swiss cheese with literally hundreds of holes staring back—some of them with eyes. Some of them with tongues. Some of them with penises or knives going in or out. All of them oozing or crying or bleeding and blotting the napkin—spelling out the words *San Francisco*.

"It was as if I'd just found a scorpion crawling across my hand.

"It scared the shit out of me.

"I shook it loose. I opened the car door and actually kicked it out in the street. I didn't even want to touch it.

"I mean I knew something was wrong with him.

"I stepped on the gas and speeded away from there as fast as possible.

"I thought maybe I should call the police but what could I report? That some guy was crying over a piece of Swiss cheese?

"Christ, look at me—I'm still trembling and sweating. I get

that way every time I think about it. And yet I don't mean to scare you—just prepare you for what's ahead. And yet you still don't know what I'm talking about, do you? A smart man like you? A writer like you?

"A man fluttering through time and talking about *nature*?

"God what a joke!" he suddenly laughed at me in the rear-view mirror. "How stupidly romantic you are!" he said and stepped on the gas as if he were still trying to get away from those doodles.

As if he *had* been stung by a scorpion.

"Don't you see?" he snapped angrily, like a teacher to his pupil. "Don't you understand that some people are meant to fill each other's holes—but usually these people are men and women? And usually these people just accept who they are!"

His words seemed to turn on me, like a reflection.

"Just wait till you've been here awhile," he said even louder. "Just wait till you finally put Florida behind you and confront your own black holes—your enormous inner spaces. You're in for some rude awakenings, my palindromic friend. I don't give a shit where you came from. I don't give a flying fuck what you think you are," he shouted—and I didn't like the tone of his voice at all.

It seemed to surround me. It seemed to accuse me.

He swerved furiously around a corner and I couldn't help feeling instant relief when I spotted a sign saying HYDE STREET.

"You better listen to me because I'm here for a reason," he said with new speed—and new venom.

"You better hold on because you're in a time machine now," he said.

"I'm telling you anything can happen here," he said.

"I'm telling you it doesn't matter which shapes you've held before—be it man or woman or devil or dog, you're going to meet a new one here.

"There are all sorts of strange and exotic species in this garden, buddy—and most of them have holes. And all of them have tongues.

"And some of them masturbate in front of mirrors.

"And nothing is what it appears to be—not even me.

"Certainly not you.

"Not even the words *San Francisco.*

"So wake up!" he suddenly shouted at the top of his lungs. "It's a whole new ball game and you're up to bat!" he said as he slammed on the brakes. "And it's *your* balls that are gonna get batted around!" he shrieked and laughed and came screeching to a halt in front of the number I had given him.

It was 1881—a palindrome.

A three-story building standing on a corner.

I looked at it and could see myself looking back in the cab window.

I fumbled for my wallet. I dropped my blank notebook on the floor. I asked him how much I owed. He was still laughing.

Except it was a dark laugh. A devilish laugh.

Now it was my turn to get nervous.

"Listen," I said as I reached for a ten-dollar bill and tossed it over the front seat. "Listen," I said instinctively, throwing the same profanities back at him, "I don't give a damn how many platitudes you picked up in this cab. I don't give a fuck how many palindromes you can recite in your mind. I think you're full of shit. If you've got a college education—if you belong to a fucking *fraternity*—then what the hell are you doing driving a cab?"

I felt like an animal lashing back, probably out of fear.

All I could think about was getting out of there.

All I knew was I had sublet an apartment from a couple I had talked with on the phone. Yes, I was clean. Yes, I would gladly take care of their cat while they were in Europe. Yes, I would be happy to send a deposit. Yes, I understood they would be gone by the time I arrived and the woman down the hall would manage everything. She was quite attractive, they said. Very sweet and very dependable, they said. She would be happy to show me around, they said, and suddenly I couldn't wait to get inside. Suddenly this cab driver was too much for me—too intense and too dark for me. I was convinced he had purposely mixed his metaphors and completely made up the story of the mad doodler. I was certain he was trying to fuck my mind the way he said others would fuck my body. I knew he was leading me toward a specific point and I didn't want to hear it. I reached for the door handle.

He reached for my arm.

His hands were so big.

It happened so fast.

They locked like a vise and he looked me right in the eyes.

At first I thought he was angry. At first I thought he would furiously try to defend himself against my words. At first I tried to pull myself away.

And then I realized if he let go I'd drown.

Everything somehow changed with his touch.

It seemed to grow stronger—it gradually hurt—and yet it was pulling me up and actually out of myself.

I could see calendar pages storming all around me. I could feel the Florida surf pounding savagely inside me. I could see his eyes getting darker and nearer as his mouth opened and millions of tiny fish started feeding on my body.

Suddenly nothing was real except a meeting of flesh.

I knew one day I'd know the doodler *did* exist.

I knew how foolish I had been to question or doubt or even to pay him.

I watched him open his mouth as if to speak and then to kiss.

I couldn't believe it.

I blinked my eyes.

I took several steps through broken glass and heard it echoing in his hot breath.

Rumbling in my typewriter.

"There's just one more thing," he said very slowly. "Just one more very important thing," he said very gently. "I read it once in a newspaper column and someday you'll understand what it means," he whispered like a lover. "*San Francisco is a peninsula,*" he said. "*It's surrounded on three sides by water and on one side by reality.*"

And with that he suddenly let go of my arm and exploded *again* into laughter. Deep, ugly, haunting—horrible laughter. Laughter that literally flooded the air and capsized me instantly and brutally into despair. It was as if he had purposely let me go—to watch me drown. I could see his dark eyes hovering above, as if on a cliff, looking back at me.

As if in a doodle.

His laughter thundered. It not only entered itself, but devoured itself—actually seemed to fuck itself; implode in and then out of itself. I had no choice but to reach for the door handle.

I forgot completely about my blank notebook.

I reacted totally out of impulse and my instinct for survival.

I yanked on the handle and pushed with my shoulder and reached for my suitcase and went sweeping out of his cab all in the same motion. All in the same shudder. And then I saw Julian.

I couldn't believe it.

I blinked my eyes.

I took several steps through broken bottles and heard them echoing in shadows. And didn't know where I was.

And didn't know *when* I was.

It was as if I *had* stepped out of a time machine and saw Julian heading toward me. Directly toward me.

When had he turned around? Why hadn't I seen it?

What the hell's going on here?

There's just too much to tell—too much about sex. Too much about fluorescent lust and eventual love. And peninsulas.

And tongues.

And the woman who was waiting inside that palindrome.

One thing at a time, I tell myself. You mustn't go too fast, I tell myself. Keep it moving in a straight line, I tell myself. Julian will be here any minute, I tell myself. Light another cigarette, I tell myself. A penis is a peninsula, I tell myself.

The only side to reality is the inside, I tell myself.

And yet I know there are no straight lines—only spirals. Only reversed directions. A shadow—light's echo; an echo—sound's mirror. *Evil—live*'s palindrome. I have no choice but to turn back through broken images and make you understand the panic—the brutal thought of exposure—of coming face-to-face with Julian.

I felt more naked than in a locker room.

I made an about-face on splintered glass.

I headed into my own shame as I turned away from Julian.

As I raced down the street and remembered the woman named Anna.

It was an instinctive reaction—my mind's attempt to escape like my legs. Or to echo like my footsteps.

Or to lap like tongues at wounds.

She pronounced it gently, with a soft *a—Anna*. She offered me her smile with her hand. She saw I was out of breath and made me sit down. And made me some tea. She was tall with dark hair and wide hips and eyes much too close together. And yet she *was* attractive. Mainly because of her soft voice and swollen tits. Mainly because of the *way* she introduced me to Digit the cat and Beulah the bird. "Digit has been waiting to meet his temporary master," she giggled, "but Beulah belongs to me." The "me" seemed to apologize for itself. It seemed to stand up and bow in on itself—as if to forgive itself—and yet it swallowed the entire room. And then it started asking me questions.

At first the standard *who-you-are* and *what-you-do* and *where-you-are-going* questions.

And then the *Where-do-you-stand-on-abortion?* questions.

And then the *Do-you-like-to-sail?* questions.

And then the *Have-you-ever-been-married?* questions.

And then the *Why-did-you-move-here?* and *Who-did-you-leave-behind?* questions.

And then the ultimate question—the much-too-direct question—the never-expected-to-hear-yet-had-already-been-asked-by-the-cab-driver question *Are you gay?*

It seemed to slip itself into the conversation. It was asked much too casually. It came from lips that remained parted and waited for an answer. I had given her my entire life as if it were an interview and now she wanted my soul. And yet I was determined not to lie. That was the reason I had moved here. That is the reason I sit here at my typewriter and look back as if at all women.

And answer as if to God.

"Yes," I can hear myself saying. "No," I can hear myself saying. "Goddamnit, what the hell does it matter?" I can hear myself saying. "Is that what you want from me—my sex? My dick? Are you worried I can't stick it?" I can hear myself saying.

"Is that what a *man* is?" I can hear myself saying.

I purposely threw that word at her as if it were an object.

I didn't mean to yell but I did mean to aim and I watched it strike its mark, hitting her between the eyes, causing those eyes to open wide and actually move farther apart, making her more beautiful.

Making her almost radiant.

Causing her to smile and instantly to disarm me with that

smile as she petted the cat and stroked the perfect order of her tiny apartment and suggested I take off my clothes.

"You've had a long trip," she said. "Why don't you relax here for a while before I show you your apartment?" she said. "It's almost New Year's Eve and I've got some champagne in the refrigerator," she said. "Why don't I draw you a bath?" she said.

"Why don't I pour us a glass?" she said.

Her eyes were like bright stars, staring back over her shoulder as she disappeared between beaded curtains and then I noticed a copy of *Playgirl* magazine on the end table. And then I noticed a marijuana plant growing in the far corner beneath Beulah's cage. And then I laughed out loud and closed my eyes and realized there was a bulge inside the blue denim of my pants. And then the doorbell rang.

And then I saw the cab driver.

And then he saw my bulge.

And then I saw my blank notebook in his hand.

And then nothing was real—because everything was *too* real.

Because Anna was kissing my eyes.

"You're in a dream," she said. "Open your eyes.

"You're with *me* now," she said.

And then the doorbell rang. It was Julian. I quickly covered my electric typewriter. I purposely hid these words in a drawer. I got out my tape recorder but didn't tell him it was on. We sat at the table in front of my sliding glass doors and talked about little things. About how damp and how cold everything was. About how old everything was. Julian suggested we smoke a joint.

And then she was groping, actually stroking through blue denim as her lips moved from eyes to chin, from chin to neck, forever downward as she reached inward, as if into a drawer.

"I once caught my father masturbating," Julian said. "He didn't know I was watching. I was only thirteen and had just discovered the act myself. Used to do it three or four or even five or six times a day, usually in the bathroom. I kept telling my mother I had diarrhea. All I had to do was put my hands in my pockets and it got hard. All I had to do was look at my penis and it got hard—just at the thought of it. Every time I peed I started rising and peeing all over the floor and the seat and even the urinals at school. One day I looked over and saw I wasn't the only one who got hard. And then I saw my father.

"I don't know why I'm talking about it now," Julian said, "except it somehow seems important. It somehow belongs here, in this image I have of myself with you. Before that day I was a child. Even when I masturbated I was innocent in my eagerness to explode. But when I saw it in my father's hands it took on new weight—almost an urgency. His penis was so large and his muscles were so tight and his entire body was straining and pulling so hard to pump the satisfaction out of himself that I felt betrayed. For the first time in my life he wasn't my father or my mother's husband, but a man. He was reaching inside himself. It had nothing to do with me or with the shape of the thing I called family. I trembled at the sight of him.

"I couldn't help getting hard myself.

"It was the last moment of my childhood," Julian said. "My mother and brothers were out. I was supposed to be at a friend's house. My father was in the bedroom, standing in profile in front of the mirror where my mother usually dressed. His pants were down around his knees. His shirt and tie were still on. His eyes were locked inside the glass. I could see him through an open doorway. I could watch him watching himself, holding himself, becoming more and more involved with himself as if he were with another person. It was the strangest thing to see this hand which had hovered over my childhood—which had shaped my entire being—suddenly reaching through shirttails and holding so monstrous a purpose. With me it had always been a boyish game, an attempt at instant excitement behind closed doors. But with him it was clearly *sex*, some immense manly involvement that needed an entire empty house. There was no need to close his bedroom door.

"I stood in the hallway watching and reaching with my own hand.

"You must understand what my father was like," Julian said. "If anybody he was Ward Cleaver on 'Leave It to Beaver.' I always hated that show and yet he always made us watch it. That and 'My Three Sons' and 'Father Knows Best.' Somehow the parents in these shows always struggled and triumphed like he intended to do. I mean he had his own little insurance business and his own little secretary and his own little car and his own little family. And he lived in his own little house which was on its own little street which was surrounded by other streets which were named after trees or famous presidents. And he always called my mother 'dear' and he always addressed me as 'son' and he always came home for lunch and he always inspected our hands before dinner and he never failed to come upstairs and say—but not kiss us—goodnight.

"Do you see what I mean?" Julian said. "Everything around me had perfect order—a perfect harmony. Men were men and women were women and mother had father and father had a purpose which was evident everywhere in our lives. Even on TV. Especially when we went to church. Parents did not have sex—they had children. They did not have desires—they had communions. Everything made sense; everything remained pure—almost sanctified—until the moment I caught my father masturbating.

"Until the instant I reached for my own sex.

"I know I'm a little stoned right now," Julian said, "but you must allow me this space to talk about it. And to look back through time at it. Because when I say I reached for my own sex, I mean just that—my *own* sex. The male sex. The shape in my hand. The shape of my father. The motion in the mirror. That moment in a doorway.

"You!" Julian said.

"Myself!" Julian said.

"The container I had come from!" Julian said. "The motion that had made me!" Julian said.

"Don't you see?" Julian said. "I was masturbating *with* him. I was turning toward the mirror and shooting, too. We were having our own communion. I was looking at him and yet knowing it was me exploding through a penis, and spilling onto the floor, and splattering into images—and dripping down the glass.

"And wondering what if my father had been *here*, instead of with my mother, at the moment I was conceived? Where would I be *then*? Who was that on the mirror *now*? It was too ridiculous to imagine—and yet too real to escape. I was only thirteen.

"I'm now nearly thirty.

"Everything has changed.

" 'Leave It to Beaver' is off the air.

"Ward Cleaver is dead. He shot himself into a mirror.

"He wiped himself off with a handkerchief.

"I disappeared down a hallway, out the back door, into my manhood—all in the same motion.

"All in the same memory.

"That night before dinner, when my father inspected my hands, it was as if we were touching dirty secrets.

"That night before bedtime, for the first time in my life, I asked him to kiss me.

"And then I grew up," Julian said.

"And then I met you," Julian said.

"It's all the same moment," Julian said.

"I'm in the same mirror," Julian said.

And then she was laughing, laughing and licking and reaching inside; and opening me up; and pulling me out; and taking me in; and moaning and squeezing and licking and biting and trying to breathe through long hair—pressing fingers along my chest and knees against my toes and her tongue into my tender tip; then pulling and purring and giving and grabbing and kissing and lapping and loving and loving and I *had* to reach back. I couldn't help myself. I had no choice but to take Anna's head in my hands and slow it down, control its motion—or else explode within seconds.

"Take it easy," I remember whispering. "This moment belongs to both of us.

"I *want* you," I remember whispering.

And then she was laughing, laughing and leading me to the bathroom—to a sunken tub that was flanked by mirrors. It could easily have accommodated four, maybe even six, and right away I noticed an ice bucket and two glasses already set up on a stool beside it.

And then she closed the door.

And then she lit some candles.

And then she switched off the light.

And then I realized this was a way to put Florida behind me—really *behind* me—by putting it into her.

By thrusting it deep inside.

By entering myself as a *man*.

And then we were bobbing—bobbing and splashing and toasting and touching toes underwater—and her tits really *were* like life preservers. They seemed to hold her up. They caught the candlelight and illuminated her face and the dark curls around her forehead. They tucked the water around themselves—around hard nipples and inside soft curves that ebbed and rose and squeezed and fell and swelled inside her ripples.

And the mirrors multiplied it all.

They made our tiny tub seem like a vast ocean.

They turned a few flickers of light into a universe of burning suns.

God, what a sight! The world was suddenly transformed. The water was so warm—it melted away my shell. It made me feel so good.

It made me get so hard.

It made me reach out and pull those tits and her arms and her shoulders into me—into *my* embrace—as she held on, looked up, opened her lips, admitted my tongue and reached with thighs down below. So completely.

So excited by everything that surrounded us.

At one point I couldn't help just squatting in the water and letting her float over me—letting her gradually descend down and up on me—and at that moment I realized how much I had learned about fucking with woman by having fucked with man. I mean the sense of power and position. I mean, I think, the simple fact that there was a hole where it was supposed to be. It was so easy to enter—so perfectly prevailing! I could hold her and turn her and position her and actually enter her as if she were a book, a blast of my imagination—a tug on my consciousness as well as my sex. At another point I reached down through the water and cupped the inside of her thighs and spread her apart and let my fingers slide into that separation which brought us together. "That's it," I whispered. "You fuck me with your cunt."

I looked her right in the eyes when I said it.

I tried to make her understand that "cunt" was the most loving word I could come up with.

I could see how much she loved the idea of it—of *her* having the power. Of her *leading* the thrust.

I could feel my dick fitting perfectly into her perspective.

It was her idea that we go into the bedroom.

She proposed it in a toast and immediately we giggled and

grabbed for towels and started pushing each other through doorways.

I had a hard-on all the way down the hall. We shot past windows and I imagined all sorts of people looking in at us. But Anna just laughed. She said nobody was watching but I knew somebody was. I could feel eyes like a hot breath on me. I had visions of sirens converging and policemen catching us in our contortions, announcing it to the neighborhood, and I still didn't lose my hard-on. We rushed inside the bedroom and dropped our towels and leaped on the bed and the whole thing became mindless.

We entered our separate bodies utterly.

We held and beheld each other ferociously.

Her cunt had its own juices—a life I had never really considered.

It was as much a mouth as a cunt, and I could swear there was a tongue moving around inside. I told her she was eating me up. I told her to please stop or I'll come. I begged her to please stop or I'll come. Our faces were just centimeters apart and we both tried to hold our breaths and stop our motion and I could feel her slow, hot, heavy exhale pouring over my ear my neck my shoulder my God *she's* coming, I thought. She's *coming*, I thought, and the thought was too much for me.

I snapped back to my senses.

I saw Julian over my shoulder.

I heard Julian in my tape recorder.

I raced down the street and kept turning around.

And kept fucking Anna.

She was squeezing and seething with excitement.

Yes, *seethe*—that's the word that gets it all. The streets as well as the ripples. The shadows as well as the thrusts.

It comes from the Old English word for "rage."

It means, literally, "to soak or saturate in liquid." Or: "to be in a state of rapid agitated movement." Or: "to churn or foam as if boiling." Or: "to suffer violent internal excitement."

And she wouldn't let me go.

She locked her legs behind me.

She wrapped her arms around me.

She pressed a tear against me.

I couldn't take it anymore.

I couldn't hold it anymore.

I had no choice but to explode inside and turn around and *face* Julian.

And embrace the *thought* of Julian.

And accept the *shape* of Julian.

And tear Anna off me, and throw Anna away from me, and put myself *there*, on those streets, in those shadows—in that present as well as the presence of Julian.

No matter how awful it was.

No matter how terrible or transformed I was yet to become.

It had been years since my encounter with Anna. So much had happened between then and this moment on asphalt. It just didn't make sense to keep remembering it now.

But Julian was gone.

Gone as certainly as Anna was gone.

Swallowed by the night or by the neon light of a porno shop.

It had happened so fast.

I had just heard his footsteps.

I had just turned around.

I had just stepped through glass.

Everything was broken—even the truth.

Not just its reflection.

It didn't matter which mirror I looked at; it didn't matter which perspective I suddenly strapped myself into—the machines in motion or the machinery of Anna, they all turned themselves toward this moment.

Toward that porno shop.

It stood like a prostitute in the middle of a drab block.

Its painted sign was burning neon, flashing sex, screaming HARDCORE! HARDCORE! HARDCORE! HARDCORE!

All its windows were painted black as mascara.

I took my first steps cautiously, at a snail's pace, wanting Julian to be inside—and yet afraid that he would be inside.

I crossed over that doorway carefully, as if I were stepping on forbidden ground—as if I were entering a new sex.

Inside the light was fluorescent.

The walls were lined with flesh.

The cash register was surrounded by dildos.

A life-sized rubber sex doll was sitting naked on a filing cabinet, its mouth open, its legs spread, its breasts inflated—its bloated hands holding a sign saying THREE ENTRANCES TO PLEASE YOU.

There were at least a dozen customers in the shop—all men. All alone.

All of them moving from one magazine to the next—from one dirty book to another—from *WHIP ROD* to *LESBIAN LIFE* to *HARD LOVE* to *TEASING TEENS* to *TORTURE BOUTIQUE*.

But I didn't see Julian.

The man behind the counter snapped on a radio. It was blaring an old Beatles' song: "All you need is love . . ."

But nobody seemed to notice.

They were too busy devouring *GANG-SEX* or *MOUTH-FULL* or *SEX FREAKS* or *LONELY WIVES* or *HOW TO EN-LARGE YOUR PENIS*.

They were too busy taking those fantasies off the shelves or stuffing them into their minds (or puffing them out in their pants) and they didn't look at me. And they didn't look at each other.

At least not in the eyes.

That was one of the first things I noticed.

There weren't any couples and nobody came in pairs and I didn't see any women and I didn't hear any giggles and everything seemed so serious. And the windows seemed so black.

Day or night didn't matter.

The weather inside never changed.

All the sex was frozen.

The walls were all in motion.

These men were here like me—solitary in their sex and aroused in their minds.

Reaching for something alive—yet holding only images as they moved from the books to the magazines.

From the magazines to the counter.

From a jar of LOVE LUBE to a tube of PROLOONG to an issue of SWINGER to a copy of THE *ANAL*YST to a man coming down the . . .

The stairs!

How had I missed it?

Why did he have a bulge in his pants?

Instantly my eyes fell on a sign I hadn't noticed—yet couldn't possibly have missed. It said PEEK SHOWS 25¢ and an arrow pointed upward.

And his bulge pointed downward.

And my hands were reaching inward, searching for some quarters, hesitating for just a moment, making sure I was ready for Julian.

Making sure I was ready for *whatever* I might find up there.

And then I took my first steps upward—upward and backward and inward and onward through glass; into the past; back to the locker room and forward in my mind to a time when Julian and I would one day sit beside sliding glass doors and reach with dirty hands toward dark secrets that eventually would explain what had driven us here—to this city; up these stairs; toward that peek-show room where Julian now waited like some monstrous sexual giggle to inhabit me forever.

I felt like Alice tumbling toward Wonderland, falling and rising at once—and yet I could never have called it love.

Fluorescence hovered at one end of my tunnel and complete instinct at the other.

I knew Julian was up there. I could sense him like danger.

I was blinded by darkness.

It took my eyes several moments to adjust to the very dim lights which hung like distant moons over the entrance to each booth—and even longer to realize it was black curtains that gave a shadowy echo to the vague shapes which slipped inside.

Nothing in that room had substance. Everything was illusion except for the sporadic *clink!* of a quarter and the steady hum of a machine responding to it.

And so I did the only thing that made sense to me—I stepped through some curtains.

I entered a booth.

I huddled inside and waited for Julian to drop like a coin through the dark folds of my imagination.

I was certain it would happen.

I *decided* it would happen.

I decided there was only one way to find Julian and that was to let Julian find me.

And so I inserted a quarter.

And the machine got excited.

And an image shot to life.

And a man was reaching for a man reaching for a woman.

And all of them were naked.

And they were covering each other with an oily lotion on a red blanket on a sunny day on a flat expanse of ocean that looked somewhat like Florida.

A hand was touching a thigh.

A tongue was licking its lips.

A penis was getting hard.

The camera was pulling back.

A wave went crashing helplessly onto the shore.

Nobody was saying anything.

Even the ocean was quiet.

There wasn't any sound—only the steady hum of my machine.

Only the camera heading silently between the woman's legs.

And then a hand.

And then a tongue.

And then the tip of a penis.

And then a *click!* as my machine blacked out. So I reached for another quarter and realized I was hard. And realized I wanted more. And realized my heart was beating very fast. And knew I was being taken over as completely by this machine as I was by the machines in the gym. As I was by Anna. As I was by the cab driver. I could feel the constant sweep of shadows outside my curtains. I could hear the distant moans of men in other booths. I got so excited that I couldn't help reaching for my own sex and I was just pulling it out and I was just putting in another quarter when something happened so fast that I didn't know what it was until the images flashed back to life and I knew I wasn't alone.

And I figured it had to be Julian.

And I suddenly started to panic.

And I quickly realized that powerful arms were reaching from behind.

Reaching from the future.

Wrapping around and pressing against and pressing inside—actually holding me and hurting me and:

"Don't be afraid," I heard him say.

"You're not like the others," I heard him say.

"Look at that cunt," I heard him say.

"Just let me hold you," I heard him say.

"We belong here together," I heard him say.

And then grab.

And then push.

And then take my sex in his hand.

And my chest in his arms.

And my ear in his mouth.

And then thrust me again and again against that screen—against that enormous flashing fuck as if he were trying to make me part of it—as if he were trying to hurl me into it.

As if he had been planning it moment by moment.

As if he were letting me know what pain meant—what pornography meant.

What future meant.

"You're not like the *others*," I remember I heard.

"We belong here *together*," I remember he said.

"Just let me hold you. Don't be afraid. Look at that cunt.

"*Look at that cunt!*"

It is a moist spring night and the garden is alive and Digit is still with me. I inherited him, in a sense. The couple returned from Europe early, in a flurry of bad feeling, throwing accusations like knives and poor Digit was right in the middle of it. He apparently had been an anniversary gift from him to her and he didn't stand a chance. Neither of them wanted any living reminders of a romance that was rapidly dying—that was actually bleeding and then rotting all around us. The man became moody and silent, yet awesome and threatening like an avalanche. The woman moved through the apartment as if on scissors that severed everything. We had no choice but to put up with one another, at least for a time. Digit retreated to me as if for sanctuary. He huddled between my legs and slept at the corner of my bed and all I had to do was uncover my electric typewriter for him to leap on the desk and wrap himself around it as if it were something alive—something that fulfilled a need. Maybe it was its electric purr. Or maybe it was just the fact that I sat there for hours on end, recording my every impression of this city surrounded by surges, pressing keys into feelings and feelings into words that caused Digit to purr back—to lap his paws and lick the pauses that occasionally pulled me up and out of myself; that made me reach out and stroke him and tell him in words out loud that I had finally found us a place of our own, an oasis with a garden—an escape from the asphalt and litter boxes of this section of town. "You're about to be free," I remember whispering to him late one night, knowing he had never set foot outside the framework of their existence. "There's an entire world out there," I remember telling him, then watching him turn and stretch and rise and look back across my typewriter so innocently—and yet instinctively wide-eyed, as if across an open field that would create itself through me. As if there were a breeze, not just a promise issuing from my breath.

And yet the apartment remained a battlefield. Both of them refused to retreat. It would be a month before my new apartment would be vacant and I had no choice but to stand between them. They dug themselves into their emotions as if into trenches—as if for a final battle. Even Anna kept her distance from our door, which was a relief to me. She had hounded me for months, always inviting herself in, always seeming to hurt for more of me—sometimes taking on the aura of a leper as she presented her womanhood like a sore for me to soothe with the miracle of sex. I don't know how else to explain it. I don't know if it was pity or perversion which made me hold her as if to heal her—which drew me to her again and again, until the couple finally returned with the broken souvenirs of their relationship. Until the night the woman had a date and somebody else came by to pick her up.

For the first time, for an entire night, we were in that apartment alone—this moody man and me. And Digit. And a bottle of tequila which the man consumed in straight shots, in fierce gulps, one right after another, until he got sick and threw up in the toilet. And then he came out and stood in the doorway and started telling me about the Arab on the beach in Venice, the Arab who had caught her eye—the opium and the hashish and the night of evil splendor. And then he looked at me long and hard with red eyes and immense bags that made him seem so helpless, so weighted down against the door, so exposed and naked and ashamed at having it show. His avalanche had melted into tears I couldn't ignore. There was no way for me to pretend I didn't know what he was talking about. I looked at him as if at someone performing an autopsy. I hated him for reminding me of my own mortality and yet I loved his vulnerability—the strength of his weakness as he confronted the viscera of their relationship. He had nothing more to lose and nothing left to show. And nowhere left to go. It seemed as natural as petting the cat. I stepped toward him as he toward me. It was my wildest fantasy come true. I was embracing a man who was embracing the thought of his woman embracing another man. In this city of reflections. No longer was I an innocent bystander or a civilian casualty or even a seeker of sex. Something else happened.

Something much deeper—something much truer.

Something which made me a part of it.

I looked back and looked up and held on and it was as if I were embracing light itself. Suddenly there was no such thing as flesh or fixed attributes or even macho images. They were just illusions perpetuated by love. They were just photographs taken by the heart! I can't even recall who touched first, or who undressed whom, or even how we ended up on that bed together. Or even when the woman burst in on us. How much had she seen before we heard her scream? Everything happened so fast. The images kept changing. One moment I was drowning and the next moment I was flying. And the next moment I was being sucked in as if by gravity. Nothing stood still. There is no way to stop it even now. I cannot frame it or explain it like art—but only contain it like matter contains atoms. To isolate even one breath of that fury is to rob it of the only thing it was—motion! A constant sweep! A woman's scream! A man reaching for a man springing naked and erect from a blanket. Into the light. Onto a beach. All in a flash. As if in a dream. As if in a peek machine. And then the camera pulls back.

And the lights flash on.

And a voice shouts, "Closing time!"

And I wake up.

And I look up.

And I see Julian.

And I hear other shapes scurrying like cats to get out of there, out of the other booths, away from the splashing light that allowed no dark corners.

That dispelled all images.

That moment was a collision. An auto at an intersection. You see it coming and you slam on your brakes and you know you can't avoid it and you know it is already happening and you say "Oh shit" or "Good God!" because you have no choice but to accept it. Accept *what you are at that moment.* A spark in time! A culmination of everything you can ever be! That's why you look back and linger as if endlessly and see your entire life at one fatal glance—because *you know you are falling in love.* Because you can never turn back again.

Julian was as inevitable as the woman's scream. Both of them exploded into light. Both of them sent me scurrying out into streets. I was halfway down the block and I was running out of breath and I had already flagged down a cab and I was just getting inside when Julian caught up and eased in beside me and was hardly out of breath at all. He just acted as if he belonged with me. He didn't say a word. He waited for me to give the cab driver my address. He reached out and put his hand over mine, as if to steady me. As if to quiet me. My first impulse was to give a fake address and make a break for it as soon as we reached familiar territory. But then I saw him smile, and then I remembered the gym, and I knew I would see him again, and possibly again and again, and suddenly it was too good to be true—even my fear! Even my despair. (Who was it who said everything alive wants to exist, even the iridescent orchid or amoeba—even the suicide in midair?)

I'm trying to tell the truth now. I'm everywhere in time now. I'm here with you and I'm there with Julian and I'm out of that apartment with my suitcase in one hand and Digit in my duffel bag, his head sticking out, his body zipped in, his eyes frantically questioning where in the hell we were going. Even I didn't know. I felt so bad, yet so glad it was over, as if after the lingering death of a friend. For the first time, for an entire month, I was without my prearranged transitions—without order or outlets to plug in my electric typewriter: a castaway on the currents of the city.

A tiny surfer atop the crests of radio waves.

It didn't matter if I was looking at a portrait in a museum or a painted lady on the streets; it didn't matter if it was the scent of seafood from a fine restaurant or the smell of vomit in a dark doorway—they all contained an art. They all sent me hurling like cable cars through the crowded fury of my imagination. Even the cheap apartment house where I rented by the week contained a kind of magic. Its torn curtains and wilting wallpaper were already forming themselves into words. Its dark hallways and dirty toilets contained holes like eyes that watched as if from the future. It was the kind of place where a novel is born—or a suicide discovered. The man in 412 was blind, yet he always wore binoculars around his neck. The woman in 420 was really a man, yet in the middle of every night I could hear her praying the rosary out loud. Her corduroy voice sawed through walls as thin as pages. During the day I sometimes caught her heavy perfume lingering like a prostitute in the hallway. I moved in and out of elevators as if inside parentheses—or as if between lines (where all real writing is done)—and realized that not just my life, but the building itself—maybe even the city itself—was performing a kind of penitence. As if in a kind of . . . purgatory.

Even Digit didn't purr for that entire month. It was as if he sensed he didn't belong there—knew he couldn't survive there. I had had to sneak him inside since they didn't allow animals of any sort. Not even birds in cages. "Not in this section of town," the manager had told me. "We have enough animals already." But Digit was now a part of me, an extension of me, and I had no choice but to contain him like an emotion. Hold him like a secret. Keep him more personal than a prayer. Promise him a garden, or a universe, or the heavens—and the eventual return of the typewriter that made him purr.

The one I had so carefully shipped from Florida.

I remember the day I went to retrieve it from the couple.

It was the same day I moved into my garden apartment.

It was precisely two years and two months before the night I was to meet Julian.

It was the week before I would first go to the gay baths.

At last everything is falling perfectly into perspective!

I remember inserting my key into the outside door. I decided I wouldn't ring the bell. I figured the element of surprise was on my side. It didn't matter what I would find up there because I was prepared for anything—even the possibility of their corpses rotting into the woodwork. Or had the woman left the man? Or had the man stormed out on her? Or had they both moved out and taken my typewriter with them? I played out the scene a hundred different ways in my mind—and in my dreams. One night I saw them stabbing each other with knives. (Another night I saw it was dildos!) I should have contacted them weeks earlier and put an end to these nightmares, but it somehow seemed important for me to wait until my new apartment was ready—or until *I* was ready—and then take the stairs two at a time: march right in—explode in and then out with my typewriter. If no words were spoken, all the better.

But what I found in that apartment was beyond anything I could possibly have imagined. (When I told Julian about it years later, all he could say was: "How clever of life to imitate art!") The first thing I noticed was Beulah, in the late-afternoon light, in a corner. And the marijuana plant growing beneath her cage. And flowers on the table. And a sweet order hovering like a perfume in the air. And right away I thought I was in the wrong apartment—but my key had fit. And my body had entered. And my mind was suddenly taking in the heavy voice of . . . the man. And the unmistakable giggles of . . . Anna! I could hear them coming from behind the closed door where I had slept—where I had left my electric typewriter on a table. In a far corner. In a room now flooded with whispers. It was as if the apartment itself were talking, telling me what had happened—and that it was happening still. It said I should get out of there, go back down the stairs, ring the bell and start all over again. Let them know I was there. Change what would happen. Or else go back to Florida, or forward to Digit, and forget the damn typewriter. Forget the damn truth!

But there was no turning back. I had already given the cab driver my real address. We were moving quickly through streets. Julian's hand was still on mine as I opened a door in my mind. As I slid into that room as if I were sliding between sheets and suddenly realized there were three. The man and Anna *and* the woman. All of them naked.

All of them in bed.

But how can it be?

Immediately my memory screamed, my mind flashed, and I could see myself running away with Digit in my duffel bag. And I could see Anna appearing amid the confusion, just moments after I had left—catching the man in his shame, the woman in her anger, the apartment in its fury. And I could see revolt, maybe even revenge on the woman's face as she instinctively grabbed Anna, or held Anna, or maybe kissed Anna, and then pressed Anna like an accusation at the man: a deliberate infliction of pain that suddenly transformed itself into pleasure. Into real feeling. Into a blind reeling that swept them all away.

Yes, I could see that moment in my mind as surely as I could see Julian beside me in the cab—as surely as I could see three naked bodies wrapped around each other, pressing into each other: creating their *own* shape—a new shape that took them beyond all previous limits of . . . sexploration.

Sexpectation!

And Julian knew something was happening. He sensed it in my touch.

He responded with his fingertips.

He rubbed my hand and grabbed my arm and touched my crotch and made me erect. And got me excited. And took me out of myself—or so deep into myself that that moment *was* a collision. A fatality of time! A single groping for separate passions that reached back and forth, in and out, like letters of a palindrome. Like hands to a mirror! How else do I justify what happened between that bedroom and that taxicab—the borders of an entire epoch? How else do I convince you those two years were an *acceptable* madness—at least for San Francisco? In Florida I had allowed myself only two nights a month to be "gay," and then I would drive more than fifty miles to strange bars in strange towns where I would make up different names every time I met and had sex with strangers. One night I was Johnny Hardman and worked construction. Another night I was Geoffrey W. Harper III and had a trust fund. Another night I got really drunk and said I was Holden Caulfield. The man looked back and said he was Seymour Glass. We both delighted in our separate fictions and lived them out the entire night. And groped for them the next morning. That was the only time I shed my paranoia and nearly fell in love.

I even went so far as to date and fuck women from the office, just to make things look good. But not feel good. The unspoken lies were the worst. They were the easiest to cover but the hardest to live with. But still I acquired quite a reputation. Even the society editor put the make on me. And one of the feature writers was always spreading her legs in my direction whenever she knew I had a deadline. It got to the point where I felt like Superman—always performing as if I were invulnerable. As if I were a blind, impenetrable force. But whenever I changed into my Secret Identity it was another matter. Then the humanity came through. Then the lies had meaning. Then the names I made up and the roles I took on and even the clothes I wore to accentuate them had a kind of horny honesty about them. They were designed to disguise the facts in order to satisfy the truth. In order for me to be real.

How *does* a man fall in love with a man? How do two men live together in a relationship which is usually occupied by opposite sexes—and by the promise, and then the reality, of children? How do you admit a man into your life without admitting he is in your body? How do you tell your parents you have a "husband"—or your brother he has an "in-law"—when you are always feeling like an outlaw in your simple need to have love? How dare you even ask such questions when you are driving fifty miles across the flat surface of sex? Or when you have just met a man in the peek-show room of a porno shop which your parents could never even begin to comprehend!

Now do you see? So much that hadn't even happened yet—and so much that was such a part of me that I couldn't even see it—sprang up from that bed, into that cab. As if across time. As if between legs! As if those two moments marked the extremes of my life in San Francisco—bookends to a series of sexual thrusts that took me into bars, baths, gyms, parks, cabs, apartments, streets, shadows, mirrors of my sex. Even the questions had answers that were just a new set of questions that moved back and forth, in and out of bodies, images, roles, definitions—surges and thrusts of thought. Even my writing during this period took on a peculiar kind of horniness. It came out suddenly, in spurts, several times a day, sometimes between bouts of sex, sometimes at an outdoor café where I often sat with my notebook and a glass of wine. Or a double espresso that got my blood rushing and the words flowing as if I were writing letters—yet speaking to myself. There was something about being out in the open that liberated me, that made me able to describe things—and confront things—that I had never even dared breathe in Florida. A new sense of myself, of my manhood, of my humanity, of my dick gradually began to emerge in this city, in that café, in those words and bars and baths, and in bedrooms that contained every sexual possibility—every dark doodle as if it were something I had to get through. Of course I realized it was a logical reaction to the lies I had lived in Florida—a necessary stage if ever I were to meet someone like Julian (or even create someone like Julian)—but what really bothered me was that there were so few women in this part of my life. And almost no children or old people. The neighborhood where I lived with Digit and the streets that I walked alone and even the stores where I shopped and the bars where I hung out were nearly all owned and operated, lined and defined by men as hung as me. As young and hungry as me. As muscled and sculpted and sweaty and anxious to escape their lies and define their shapes and increase the size of their own truths. *Their* lives.

Take my postman Bill. Billy Hertz. A forty-four-year-old man who had spent twenty-five of them in the Marines. An ex-soldier with a dark beard and black eyes and big shoulders and a life which had been starched as straight as creases. "It was my way of having a life among men," he told me one day at my mailbox. "In an *honorable* way," he added, picking that word as if from a tooth and flicking it onto the ground, then explaining he had never had sex with a man—and certainly not with a woman—in all of those twenty-five years. "But now I'm getting even," he said with a dark laugh which capsized into delirious giggles as he planted a kiss on my cheek and then started telling me about Halloween. About how he intended to deliver the mail in . . . "Drag," he whispered as he handed me some letters. "I'm going to dress up as a *postwoman*," he said. "One of the gals in the office loaned me her uniform and I've got this platinum blond wig and a stuffed bra and full makeup and some red sequins for my beard.

"Genderfuck!" he called it. "*Revenge*," he said. "My discharge into life!" he giggled. And two weeks later he did it. I couldn't believe it! He wore that uniform like a soldier and those tits as if they were medals as he marched down and up streets ringing bells and handing people their mail. It was grotesque—and yet captivating. His black beard was such a contrast to the blond wig. His wide shoulders seemed to burst out of that blue government-issue blouse which hung open at the neck. His hairy arms and even hairier chest just didn't belong there with long eyelashes and red lips and sequins that sparkled in the sunlight. All of what was *woman* was emphasized. All of what was *man* was acknowledged. Those two shapes seemed to do battle, and yet make love, on the same body—on the open streets. (And in front of TV cameras that followed him around that day.) How else do I describe it except as . . . bizarre. Shocking. Almost . . . sacrilegious! Like a nun lifting her long robes to show you she is wearing mesh nylons and red garters and spiked heels! All of what society thinks of as decent, as almost *holy*, was suddenly transformed into mockery, caricature, manwoman—*genderfuck* on the six o'clock news. A strange new creature seemed to twist out of its own horror and shout to the world, "*Look at me! I am all of you because I am none of you. Because I am the sum of you. Because I make just as much sense beneath my costume as you do beneath yours!*"

"*Make*" *sense*—that says it. Ears, nose, eyes, fingers, tongue—they are everything. They create the world around us—and inside us. Without them our hearts and minds would have no fuel—no fire. Musicians and artists and poets and chefs and even prostitutes (and even postmen)—where would they be without color or sound or shape or contour or size? Or thighs! (Who was it who said each of our five senses contains an art?)

You must allow me these pauses in my mind. We have been too hard on the slippery trail of Julian. So much went before, so much lies ahead—and so much comes in between. I select the moments as if I'm painting by numbers. I approach each in its turn and fill it in. But then the telephone rings, or the doorbell screams the possibility of Julian, or an image comes hurling at me from the past and I am capsized instantly into the present. A voice which doesn't belong suddenly emerges, as if through walls, and it is so immediate and so pervading that it colors everything I have yet to become with you. Or with Julian. Or with Digit.

Or with my typewriter which was still plugged in.

I raced across the room and picked it up and turned around and took a step but it wouldn't come out. It held me there, as if bound by an umbilical cord—when suddenly they saw me.

They all saw me.

They untangled themselves quickly and leaped on me instinctively and the man was so strong. And the women were so fast, like monstrous flapping birds attacking me, holding me, clawing me, tearing off my pants and mounting my shoulders and pressing me down against the floor, down against the typewriter, as my hard-on hit the keyboard and sent a flurry of letters crashing against . . . against *what*? There was no paper.

There was no purpose.

There was no Julian.

Not *then*.

Not when that moment really happened!

And yet it was as if my dick were writing what was *going* to happen—what had already happened by the time I stepped into that cab and responded to Julian's hand and unzipped Julian's pants and took Julian's sex first in my fingers and then in my mouth as the camera pulled back.

As the lights flashed on.

As the cab came screeching to a halt.

As a familiar voice suddenly shouted *"What the hell's going on here?"*

Can you see it? Can you see it happening so quickly? Can you see me pushing back and abandoning my typewriter and leaping high into the air and grabbing the woman as the man grabbed Anna as we both started pounding furiously into our separate fucks? On the same bed! Side by side. Two men fucking two women who were tools—receptacles!—since the real fury of emotion was between *us*.

Between me and this man!

Both of us *being* man.

Both of us *fucking* woman.

Both of us reaching out to each other as Anna reached out to the woman as Julian reached back to me as the lights flashed on and everything changed.

Everything suddenly happened as if underwater.

That's the only way to explain it.

I could hardly breathe.

No longer did the images flash forth like light, but they swam slowly into focus like fish.

Words were gurgles and sounds were bubbles. And feelings were currents. And that cab was an aquarium.

And the driver, I quickly realized, was the same as before—the man who feared doodles.

The man who loved palindromes!

I recognized his dark mustache.

I remembered his hot breath.

I saw his fierce eyes.

I watched him turning in slow motion, reaching across the backseat, pressing as if through syrup—as if through time—and for a moment I thought it was planned.

For a moment I thought he and Julian were in on it together.

That they had led me here.

That they had driven me here.

Right from the beginning.

Right from my first moment in San Francisco.

And now they were going to devour me.

But of course that was my fantasy.

The reality was that he didn't even recognize me—not until he saw me recognizing him.

And then he froze.

He hovered as if in suspended animation—as if in a rear-view mirror—and I could see his mind working.

His eyes squinting.

His lips twisting slowly upward, into a smile—into recognition—as he said (as if he were a character speaking to its author):

"Say, aren't you . . . the writer!"

But he didn't wait for the answer.

He *had* the solution.

It arrived like an anniversary.

Then exploded into laughter.

Then capsized into giggles.

Then stormed through that cab—back to Florida, forward to Julian—bubbling like a cauldron.

Burning like lies.

Telling me that everything I had ever been—and everything I was yet to be—was in my mind.

And in my mouth.

"Look at yourself," he seemed to say. *"Look where you're going. Look what you're doing in the backseat of a cab on a full-moon night—in the middle of a city. It's laughable! It's preposterous!*

"It's dangerous," he seemed to say—and yet he didn't say a word.

He didn't have to.

It wasn't him speaking to me—but me speaking to myself. On a moist spring night.

Looking from the future.

Listening to his laughter.

Pressing these words as if into a diary.

Trying to tell the truth.

Trying to prepare you for the words he *would* say—and eventually did say when I tossed money over the front seat and grabbed Julian by the arm and pulled him out of that cab, into the night—toward the apartment and the typewriter and the garden that was so carefully watched and protected by Digit.

So carefully tended and intended by me.

"Hey!" he cried out, and it wasn't just his words—but his body chasing us across the street.

"Hey, wait a minute! I've got something for you. I've been saving something for you!"

At last I can see it.

At last I can take you inside my relationship with Julian.

At last I have the key to unlock the past—and open up the future—and free my words—and make you understand that Julian wasn't pressing so much against *me*, but against *love*, as if it were a weight. As if it were a chamber. As if it were a force he had to overcome to build himself up stronger, make himself more powerful.

But then so empty.

As if after drugs.

A *diary*—that's it.

My blank notebook!

The one I had bought in Florida.

The one I had left in his cab so long ago.

That's why he was chasing me.

That's what he was handing me—a reprieve.

A chance to begin again.

"Here!" he said, and he thrust it into my arms. "Here, take it. It's yours!

"It's *both* of yours," he said, stealing a quick glance at Julian as he thrust it even harder against my chest—this time stabbing it there. Twisting it there. Staring with wild eyes and immense scope which made him seem like a madman. Or a demon. Or a prophet. Or a mystic taking in all of my life.

The *rest* of my life.

"*C'mon, TAKE it,*" he said.

"*This notebook is YOU,*" he said.

"*You are BEGINNING,*" he said.

And then he exploded again into laughter—into deep, ugly, haunting, hysterical laughter that seemed to rearrange itself.

Transcend itself!

One moment it was man and the next moment it was woman.

And then it was me.

And then it was Billy!

And then it was Anna.

And then it was a prayer, a dream, a *clink!*, a scream that seemed to echo down the streets and wake up the night and cause windows to open, pants to drop, waves to crash, my heart to flash blindly, electrically, like fluorescence—like neon—into Julian. JULIAN! Julian. JULIAN!

Julian.

(Who was it who said a diary is the last place you should go if you wish to seek the truth about a person?)

• • •

I am sitting at my notebook, which is on a glass-topped table, which is right next to some sliding glass doors, which open into a garden (or a yard, if you prefer), which has a fairly decent expanse of begonias, baby tears, calla lilies, fuchsias, a rosebush growing in the far corner, fog tumbling over the fence, and a birdbath. And a clothesline. And a broken-down old lawnmower left here by the last tenant. And of course a magnificent pine tree which towers over the entire garden and which seems to have a life of its own—a reflection of what's inside these sliding glass doors where two men live. This morning, for example, I saw a red bird in that tree; some days there are dozens of birds in that tree; al-

ways there are pinecones in that tree, and often the wind comes shooting down with the fog, puffing that monstrous pine so violently that I get scared. It is suddenly in spasms. It is stepping forth to attack me. I can't help the way I feel. I look out from within; I look in from without. I am without perspective. . . .

This morning, as I was saying, I was sitting in front of my sliding glass doors, sipping my coffee, smoking a cigarette, waiting for my turn at the toilet, when suddenly I remembered this notebook which has remained blank—but in the back of my mind, in a drawer of my desk—for months now. It has been waiting to be inhabited, like the empty birdhouse which hangs from that tree; or like me. . . . I can say that now because I can see now that I must address these words to *somebody: to a third party who will help me understand what has happened—and what is happening still—as I sit here watching the fog tumbling down the hillside, forever down that hillside, between these houses and over the fences which draw the lines and separate the yards and measure the spaces. And define the lives.*

Let me begin by telling you (singular? plural? who knows?) by telling you we live in a tiny apartment in the back of a house which faces the backs of other houses which have tiny apartments like ours. Or rather, mine. I'm the one who found it. I'm the one who was living here long before I ever met him. I'm the one who plants the begonias and waters the baby tears and prunes the fuchsias and steps on the snails. Yes, he moved in—but often he isn't here. Not even when he is *here. Not even when we're sitting in the garden smoking a joint and joking about having sex in front of the mirrors. The mirrors which Julian insisted I have mounted on the walls beside my bed.*

I had them installed exactly one month before we went to Mexico.

Of course you don't realize it, but I just answered the telephone. It rang three times before I got there—and then it was a wrong number. In the meantime this notebook sat empty. My time is so different from your time, whoever you are. So much can happen in the expanse of a minute—just as so much can happen in the expanse of a garden that is reflected in mirrors which are on the far side of this tiny apartment, facing the bed and the windows and the garden beyond: throwing everything back—turning outside in and inside out—multiplying the light and expanding the vision and making it seem as if I am actually living in this garden. Or as if the garden is living in me.

And yet I can't help thinking that wrong number was deliberately intended to take me away from these words—to exchange the moment and thus change the future of this page. "No," I say. "There is no Jerry at this number. There isn't even a Julian at this number. He has his own number," I say, and then I hang up. And then I pour another cup of coffee. And then I put it on my glass-topped table and take a turn at the toilet—stopping first in front of the mirrors to observe my image. And then to observe my observation. And then to tell myself I know it is true—I know there is a direct line to a part of Julian I can never reach, not even if I call it.

I remember the first time I decided to follow him. I heard his telephone ringing and I decided instantly, even before he answered it. I had never actually asked him what he does for a living—but I knew it the moment he had that phone put in.

I knew it the moment he told me never to answer it.

But now I was going to prove it to myself.

I remember we were lying on the bed. It was late afternoon. Sunlight was dissolving through the windows, echoing in the mirrors. He had his arms wrapped around my arms, his legs around my legs. He was pressing his cheek into the back of my head and his cock against my ass. It was one of those magical moments we manage to have in spite of our differences. We just lay there, fully clothed, watching the garden and talking quietly (he talks to the back of my head; I talk to the air in front of me) . . . and I like it. I like the way he holds every bit of me with every bit of him, as if he is the wrapping paper.

As if I am some precious gift.

"Relax," he says.

"I am."

"You're not."

"I'm trying."

"Don't try. Just relax," he says. "You've got to learn how to relax." He rubs my hair. He blows hot air on the back of my neck. "You tense little fucker," he says, and suddenly we're like two lovers you might find in a teen-age romance—wrestling, joking, whispering, tickling, reaching out to pet the cat. Yes, two lovers, but we're also—two men. And not really lovers because . . .

His telephone has a distinct ring. Almost a scream. It's much louder—much more deliberate than mine. It stands like a pet on one side of the apartment, waiting to respond to its master. Mine, on the other hand, is more businesslike—more mechanical. It usually carries the voice of an editor telling me an article is accepted; or a librarian telling me the book I had put on reserve has at last arrived. But Julian's actually cries out as if in alarm, as if warning of an intruder, and immediately I cringe as if my entire world—as if every quiet moment I can ever have with Julian—is about to be torn apart.

But of course I have learned to live with it. I have no other choice. Even as I sit here with you, on the morning I have retrieved this notebook, watching the fog finally disappearing with the daylight, I know it is bound to ring. I know I will hear it scream. But still I will pay no attention. Instead I will continue onward, backward, inward—and tell you what I have set out to tell you. Which is this:

Today is the day I know I am losing Julian.

Today is the day I must go back and again find Julian.

In time you will understand.

It's only ten in the morning.

We have the entire day before us.

Julian is gone now.

Julian may never be back.

That pine tree is standing perfectly still.

I have been saving this notebook for the right moment—which has just arrived. Which cannot be stopped.

Maybe I will take you to the outdoor café later.

Maybe we will have a double espresso.

Maybe I will tell you about the fight Julian and I had this morning.

Or maybe I will forget Julian and meet another man who will take me out of myself—and back inside my mirrors.

The mirrors which Julian paid for.

(He also paid for the camera and the tape recorder and that trip to Mexico. And the drugs . . .)

See what I mean? There is so much *to tell. There is so* far *to go.*

It's as if he wanted to shed his money.

It's as if he couldn't stand looking at it.

It's as if he saw me as pure—as someone willing to accept, and therefore forgive, his transgressions. . . .

(Who was it who said personality as something with fixed attributes is an illusion—but a necessary one if we are to love?)

Please bear with me. Please stand by.

I am going to write nonstop.

I don't care what comes out.

I don't care who you are.

I'm not going to let anything interrupt us—not even Brian, my neighbor, who just stepped out of his sliding glass doors. Who is now puttering in his garden which is on the other side of that fence which divides and yet touches our lives.

I'm going to tell you the truth about what happened the first time I followed Julian into that telephone.

I'm going to tell you what really occurred when we woke up from separate drugs this morning.

I'm even going to take you back to the beginning—to the very first moment I led Julian inside this apartment—and tell you what it was like before we bought the mirrors.

And after we went to Mexico.

(I can still see the maid standing at our door. I tell her my friend is taking a siesta. She hands me her smile with some towels. "Buenas tardes," *she says, as I return to Julian naked on the bed, a fan spinning above his head, the sea crashing outside the window off our balcony. It's the last afternoon of our journey, a town called Puerto Vallarta, a room of clay and brick, the sea still thick on his body. I can't help watching him. The line of his tan. His tantalizing manhood. A mosquito bite on his leg as he sleeps so deeply, so steeply. . . . I can't help savoring the thought that I have him all to myself—that there are no telephones to ring—that at any moment I can slide into his warmth and know he will respond: recognize my touch: reward my desire with a smile as he pulls me into his sleep, his eyes still closed, the loud silence of my emotion becoming an ocean locked inside a shell that will never be found. That will never have an ear. . . .)*

I followed Julian at a cautious distance. Like the night I first met him. Only this time it wasn't quite dark. He had hung up the phone and returned to me on the bed and whispered that he had to go out early that night. That's the way he always did it, with the word out*—as if that explained it. As if that were all there was to know. He insisted on keeping this part of his life secret from me—or rather secret to him—because, as he put it (and still puts it), "You've got your writing and I've got this—it's that simple."*

And that complicated.

"We're two men," he said so many times that I can't even count them. "We cannot fit into other people's perspectives. We've got to define ourselves."

And then he would drop to the carpet and do exactly fifty push-ups, counting them out loud, giving his muscles a final pump—a perfect tone—in order (I knew) to make himself more sweaty: to create a certain "smell" as well as the right look.

And what a smell Julian had. Has! Will always have. Especially during sex. Especially when we are naked and wrapped around each other in front of the mirrors. On the bed which has no frame for fear it will break. On the mattress and box springs which are low to the floor, an island on carpet, firm and yet giving—allowing no interruption to the expanse of garden in the mirrors we face. And in that smell we embrace as a part of our instinct—a way to know we are of the same species. A way for me to know I am heading in the right direction as I follow Julian down the street and realize I have those mirrors memorized—a panorama on postcard: Julian on his knees on the mattress. Me on my knees in front of him. My back to his chest. His arms wrapped around my shoulders. My arms wrapped around his arms. Our bodies like magnets, our muscles taut, our penises erect, our eyes glued to the glass—watching the light from behind. And the glow from within. And that smell of him which becomes the smell of me which inhabits everything—even tongues licking and chests heaving and nipples swelling. And mirrors not only reflecting, but containing the desire. As if they *perspire. . . .*

Do you see how much in love I was? Do you see why I had to follow him? Do you see why I had to find out if he was heading toward man? Or toward woman? Or maybe toward something more grotesque than anything I could imagine? Do you see how fiercely independent he was—and yet how necessary it was for me, too? He was right about my writing—it is *mine. He cannot have it. He cannot share in any part of it. Even these words I present to you now are ours alone—as intimate in their own way as anything I have ever shared with Julian. If he should walk in right now I would hide them. If he should beg forgiveness; if he should tell me he is sorry for last night (and for this morning); if he should try to grab me and hold me in front of the mirrors I would reject him as being too weak—too woman. Not the man I once followed into a porno bookshop.*

Not the man who once followed me into a cab.

It's true I have double standards! I know I want to take in all of him but keep some of me in sight. That is definitely part of the problem. But I also know it's what I can't have that makes me want it all the more. (Julian was right when he said last night that it's my fantasy—not his reality—that made me follow him into the twilight. . . .)

But what did I hope to discover? Certainly I couldn't go inside. And if it were a large apartment house I wouldn't even know which apartment. But no, fate isn't as friendly as that. That's why I can sit here now and watch Brian in his bathrobe, fussing so innocently over his roses as I lead you down darkening streets, through deepening shadows, up a steep and then even steeper hill, toward a tiny cottage at the end of a NOT A THROUGH STREET *where I can crouch now as I did then amid leaves—watching with ease through a window as Julian strips naked in my memory. In front of a very old man. In a pathetic little room with bright lights and flowered wallpaper covered by some extremely old photographs—probably his ancestors. Women in shawls and their men in starched collars. Hanging rigid and arranged in elaborate frames. So serious and dignified, so hard and composed—so old in their youth. So straight in their time!*

We all watched Julian undress—me through my cracked window and they through their dusty past. All of us behind glass. Even the old man, who took off everything except his wire-rim glasses. Who was bald, except for two tiny patches of white hair above each ear, like worn-out earmuffs. Whose skin was wrinkled, whose eyes were small, whose lips were pressed tightly together—etched out of age. His arms were long and bumpy with blue veins that swelled like insect bites as his hands reached for two crisp twenty-dollar bills and placed them neatly on Julian's stack of clothing, which was right beneath my window. Which made me pull back—sink into the bushes for fear of being seen—until I realized the light was so bright inside that I was perfectly invisible outside, as if this spot had been prepared for me. As if this moment had been arranged for me.

As if I were a part of it.

As if I, too, were being paid for it.

"My God!" the old man suddenly cried out, and dropped to his knees, and started touching himself. And started touching Julian, who towered at the foot of his bed—who looked back, looked down, completely naked, but not at all erect—and then started flexing his muscles. Turning in different poses. But standing in the same spot. Watching the old man reaching up from the floor, like a slave to its master, like a man to its god, reaching and touching first Julian's thick calves, and then his hard thighs, and then his monstrous hands with their layers of dead skin from pressing so many weights—so many moments. So much of me.

"My God, my God!" the old man was saying, touching, holding himself with one hand and Julian with the other. "Oh thank you for coming here. Oh thank you for being here. You're so beautiful. It won't take long. Just a few minutes. You don't know what it's like for an old man like me. Oh thank you. Oh thank you!"

And then his face was red. And he was breathing very fast. And he was smiling wide and full and bright through clean rows of perfect teeth. And his miniature eyes were getting bigger, darker, jumping crazily out of his glasses like exclamation points as Julian just looked at him, posed for him, listened to him, but didn't say a word to him.

"C'mon!" the old man shrieked. "C'mon, tighten it up! Make *it hard! Flex that chest! Squeeze that ass! Let me* feel *those muscles! Let me lick that sex! C'mon baby, be beautiful. Be* beautiful*!"*

And then he was stroking faster, and talking dirtier, and trying to make himself harder—looking down at his sex instead of up at Julian as he scolded it, squeezed it, pumped it so hard and so fast that he shook all over, as if going into spasms, but it just wasn't working.

So little was happening.

No matter how dirty he talked.

No matter how hard he squeezed.

It was getting slightly longer, maybe even thicker and heavier, but it just wasn't rising like his blood pressure. And that's when I started to worry.

And that's when he started to turn blue.

And that's when Julian noticed it, too.

And I was just getting ready to pound on that glass—to put an end to this madness—when the old man looked up and his eyes met Julian's.

And their hands moved.

And their lips touched.

And instantly the old man's entire body started rising like a penis, fleshing itself out, pressing away the wrinkles, making him seem fuller, bigger, stronger, even . . . younger!

As if he were being charged by Julian.

As if he were being transformed by Julian.

And it happened so fast.

One moment I was feeling sorry for the old man and the next moment I was feeling jealous.

And then I was feeling fear, as if something were being taken away from me: as if something were happening here that wasn't being paid for.

That couldn't be explained.

Do you see at all what I mean?

Julian was lifting him, pulling him, holding him—but exciting himself.

As if in front of mirrors.

As if they were any two men who could have chanced to meet in a glance on a beach—or at night on a street . . .

Or in a flurry of pages that now storm through the past, through the faces in glass, back to the night when we *were like this—so lost in a kiss.*

So far into space.

So pulled by the gravity of each other's first embrace that nothing else mattered except the power of Julian . . .

The hope and immense scope of being new with Julian.

I could see it in the old man's eyes.

I could see me *in the way he looked back and reached up as if in answered prayer. As if being handed a reprieve from his wrinkles.*

Even the furrows in his forehead seemed to sift themselves into sandy hair like mine.

Suddenly his muscles were growing and his juices were flowing and he was young—and he was *me—and I knew he would be willing to do anything, be anything, try anything, allow anything—even another telephone, even another country—inside that cottage with . . .*

"Julian!"

It was my own voice. I was crying out from the future.

Everybody heard it. Even Brian heard it.

Even the old man heard it. Or thought he heard it.

In the confusion even Julian wasn't sure because at that moment the old man was panting, heaving, screaming—splashing and then collapsing helplessly, like a wave, against Julian.

Against time.

As if all of his moments were exploding into one.

As if instantly he were as old as he had ever been young.

As if every muscle and fiber of his old-man body were giving out, crashing in. Releasing the wrinkles and freeing his tears and deepening the despair. Contracting even his skull—causing his hair to retreat and his glasses to fall and those perfect rows of white teeth to drop from his mouth with a deafening roar as . . .

Everybody heard it. Even Brian heard it.

He is calling to me through my sliding glass door.

He is motioning through glass. Pushing it open.

He has climbed over the fence in his bathrobe.

"Are you all right?" he is saying.

He sees me unshaved, uncombed. Beard growing through the Band-Aid on my chin.

Smoke seeping through yellow teeth.

"I thought I heard a . . ."

He has never liked Julian. He has never trusted Julian.

He notices the bed unmade, the dishes unwashed. The Quaaludes piled at the corner of my desk.

I do not pretend they aren't there.

I don't even attempt to smile.

I simply tell him I'm fine—that nothing is happening here that hasn't happened before. That I will join him in a half-hour for a cup of coffee over the fence but first I have something to finish. Something that cannot be interrupted. I hope he will understand.

I hope I am not being rude.

I thank him very much for his concern.

I reach for another cigarette.

It is almost 11:00 A.M.

Now where am I?

Now where was I?

Oh, yes—the Quaaludes. The medical variety. The kind you get with a prescription, not the kind you buy on the streets. Heaven knows where Julian gets them, but I took one just a few minutes ago. It will help me relax. It will make us more intimate. It will slow things down and let me see things more clearly. That's what Quaaludes do—and that's why they're so good during sex—because everything opens up, even the mind.

Especially the body.

In time you will understand.

My fingers are already getting numb.

I think I am right to warn you—to prepare you for what's ahead. For what's already inside.

For what is beyond my control.

I remember once when I was very young, less than five, my father was urging me to climb the ladder, to mount the wooden horse and smile for the photographer. "Go on," he said, "don't be a crybaby. Don't be a sissy." It was at a carnival which was on a boardwalk which was near a seashore and I started trembling, taking a few steps at my father's prodding and then freezing, holding on for dear life, convinced that that bucking horse was a hundred feet tall. Or a thousand feet tall. Certainly much bigger than the ferris wheel which swirled in the commotion behind it. Certainly not worth the balloon the photographer was offering me to climb aboard it. But when my father insisted—when he pushed me up another rung of the ladder and threatened me with a beating—I had no choice but to start crying. Actually screaming. Pleading to be taken down. Begging to be set free of his expectations. Knowing that being a crybaby, or even a sissy—or even getting a beating—was a lot better than being dead.

But my father just didn't see it that way.

I don't think he ever smiled at me again.

He removed me not just from that horse, but from his warmth.

"Look at Mary Kay," he said as if spitting, and then pointed

to my cousin who was younger, who was a girl, who was fearlessly climbing that horse and sitting up there like a cowboy, bouncing and laughing and kicking and waving, and looking back at me—and looking down on me—and making me feel the lessness.

And making me feel the shame.

And later, when I was much older, when my mother dug out that photo one Christmas day, Mary Kay was so surprised. She exploded into laughter. All those years I thought she had been measuring me against it and she didn't even remember it. But what really shook me—what really made me look at myself as if for the first time—was when I realized how small that horse was. How tame and how petty it was. Probably not even as big as a real one. And yet how long I had lived in its shadow . . .

And how much of the blame was my own.

And now it is true of Julian: he is so close—and he looms so big—that he scares me.

I cannot see him in perspective.

It's as if I am still a child.

I just don't have the distance to laugh.

Even that trip to Mexico is just a flicker in time away from this Quaalude. . . .

Even when I try to understand what happened when that old man collapsed; when Julian caught him and held him and carried him to the bed—and tucked him in, and kissed him good-night—all I can hear is my own scream . . .

All I can see is me *hanging on, cringing in fear, crying out to be saved from . . .*

. . . the telephone!

Julian's *telephone.*

It's ringing again.

I can hear it right now.

It's sounding like an alarm—calling me to action.

Tempting me to answer.

Why is it happening? Why at this moment?

When will it stop?

Who can it be—the old man? The sailor? The couple Julian met in a bar one night?

The possibilities are endless.

The dangers are real.

I remember that night perfectly. It was the only time I followed ahead *of Julian. Normally he talks into his telephone so quietly that I can't hear a word. But that night one slipped out a little too high, a little too loud, and it was the name of a bar. So I took a shortcut—running all the way, arriving out of breath, quickly ordering a drink and picking up a newspaper and then taking a seat in the darkest corner and pretending to read it as Julian entered alone, looked around, but didn't seem to find what he was looking for. So he sat at the bar and ordered a scotch and couldn't avoid the elbows of the man sitting next to him, who was talking to the woman sitting next to him—but who was also, I suddenly realized, rubbing his knee against Julian's knee under the bar. That's how it started.*

She was short and blond. He was tall and dark and had a mustache and big hands. Later, when the two of them led Julian from the bar to a table near mine and ordered another round of drinks, I saw the man put his hand on Julian's crotch under the table. Of course the woman knew what her boyfriend was doing. She smiled and licked his ear.

I saw the whole thing.

The man lit a cigarette and said his name was Joe.

The woman reached for the man's cigarette, taking it between long and slender fingers and arching it toward her mouth, and said her name was Mary.

Then she inhaled deeply and flicked an ash and handed the

cigarette to Julian, who used it to light his own cigarette as he laughed and said he was Jesus.

They all pretended they were getting drunk.

What happened later I don't know.

They left in a car.

So I returned home and took off my clothes and petted my cat. And then started masturbating in front of the mirrors.

Stroking faster and faster.

Going over every detail.

Imagining what they were doing.

Finally exploding, erupting—shooting all over the mirrors and the carpet and my mind in the night.

And the cat on the floor.

But what came out was not come—it was punctuation marks. It was commas and periods and exclamation points and parentheses and quotation marks. They dribbled down my leg. They oozed onto the carpet. Dashes and apostrophes and semicolons everywhere! And the last thing I remembered, just before I fell back into sleep on the bed, was the cat licking and the man asking Julian if he liked to shave cunts.

"Jesus, Joe," Julian said. "I really love to shave cunts!"

And then I woke up. It was morning. Digit was purring on my pillow. Julian's arm was around my waist. His chin was against the back of my neck and his body was pressed against mine. He had a hard-on. He was asleep. He was back. He always came back more loving—more accepting than before. More willing to lift me higher, to buy me gifts. To make me his. . . .

It was on one such morning, when I was quietly making breakfast—summoning Julian gently awake with the smell of bacon—that I decided to approach him about Mexico. Or not necessarily Mexico, but anyplace where I could have him to myself.

Where I could find out who he is without following him into bars. Or into mirrors. . . .

"Listen," I said, pouring his coffee, avoiding his eyes. "I know we're two men. I understand we can't have a relationship that is free of separateness. I realize you have to go out at night and I have to pull into myself sometimes. But let's, just for a moment—just for a week—stop and touch and look and feel and occupy the same space.

"A state of mutual *grace," I called it.*

"A chance to be in love and in touch with what we are," I said, "rather than what we cannot be.

"Listen," I said, handing him his coffee, still avoiding his eyes, realizing I was going to sound like a travel brochure—knowing I had gone over these words so many times in my mind that I had them memorized.

"Listen," I said, "let's go someplace where we can be really together for a while. I mean someplace far, like an island. Or an oasis. There's this place called Yelapa, which Brian was telling me about the other day—which seems perfect. It's in Mexico, and it's not an island but the landscape is so dense that it's only approachable by boat. No roads make it there. All the roofs are made of palm leaves turned gray and brown by the weather. There isn't even electricity. And there aren't even cobblestone streets—only dirt paths paved in dust and donkeyshit. And roosters and reptiles everywhere. Brian showed me pictures of it. It's so beautiful! Coconuts falling from trees and bananas hanging in stalks. And pineapples. And mangoes. And watermelon. And avocados. And me!" I said.

"And you*!" I said.*

"And at night," I said, "the restaurant in the village has nothing but candles in the windows. And candles on the porch. And candles on the table, other tables, an amazing glow—everyone hungry and brown from days of sunshine on the beach. . . .

"I can picture us there," I said. "I can see us there on that beach—actually in *those postcards—out of reach of telephones and traffic and newspapers and fluorescent lights. Watching the sunset and memorizing the sound of the sea late at night in a place where the stars really glow. Where there is no land-light to detract from the heavens and no big buildings to separate us from the sky! Where we'll be able to really* feel *we are part of a planet, swirling through an ocean of space and slowly expanding scope . . .*

"And hope!" I said—knowing I couldn't stop talking. Realizing this was my only chance. At last looking him right in the face and seeing his mouth hanging open, his eyes staring back . . .

His mind now awake.

"We need that," I said. "We need someplace soft—someplace gentle. Our entire landscape has been nothing but leather and concrete and neon and steel," I said. "And mirrors," I said.

"And telephones," I said.

"Images as false as teeth!" I said.

"Even our sweat seems cold as glass," I said.

"Let's get out *of here," I said. "Let's get into ourselves—into our relationship—if only for a week.*

"If only for the truth."

It was as if I had already seen what was going to happen. As if I knew how it would be once we got to Mexico. I could actually see the tiny moments, the interstices—those "nothing" spaces in our lives when we would dry our hair or take a nap and share spontaneously, naturally, even deeply. . . . But what I didn't expect was the way Julian reacted—the emotion which swelled up when my words hit him. That, it seems to me, was the real beginning of our trip to Mexico. When I saw what I thought was a tear, it vanished as suddenly in a swirl of motion which swept me away. Which carried me into the air and spun me around and then eased me to the ground as Julian just held me against him on my toes, my chin over his shoulder. My eyes facing the garden. My body enveloped as if by flames rather than arms, as if I were burning alive . . .

As if I were burning inside him.

And I knew his answer was yes.

It didn't matter that no words were spoken.

I could see it arriving with the long rays of the morning sun that spread quickly over the fence, across the garden, against the expanse of my sliding glass door . . .

Against the shape of an animal that crossed it.

It was a tiny thing, moving very slowly, leaving a slippery trail that captured the light and flared like a comet in its wake.

A universe on glass!

And yet the creature itself was transparent. It moved in a series of hurried muscular contractions which I could see as if through jelly. It tapped its way forward by frantically feeling rather than seeing with tentacles obviously blinded by the light. Wilting from the sun. Hurrying to escape its fate. Caught in the act of staying out too late—of being too long out of its shell—when suddenly it happened.

At the very moment Julian took a deep breath, the creature withered and fell.

Just as he was about to speak, the telephone rang. . . .

It is still *ringing!*

Why won't it stop?
Who can it be?

Is it the sailor? Is it the couple?

Is it the same person calling back?

Or is it Julian himself—calling himself. Knowing he isn't here. Knowing what it will do to me!

I can't stand it anymore.

I've got to get out of here.

Even the Quaalude doesn't seem to be doing anything except aggravating things—intensifying things. . . .

I'll come back to you later.

I'll take you to the café.

I'll take you to Mexico.

You'll have to excuse me.

Brian is waiting.

The old man is sleeping.

Julian put him to bed.

I saw it through glass.

Through images as high as ladders!

He retrieved the glasses. He picked up the teeth. He placed them gently on the dresser. He stood there listening to the old man panting, heaving, easing gradually into sleep before he returned to his pile of clothes on the floor and began dressing in front of my window. Adjusting himself in the glass. Looking directly at me and yet only at himself. Carefully tucking his penis into his pants, the money into his front pocket. Then stepping closer to have a better look—to comb his hair and inspect his face as if for pimples. Turning it first to one side, then the other, only inches away from my face—as if I am the mirror.

As if you *are the child!*

As if there is nothing to see except through me. . . .

And now I am back.

I have been gone almost two hours.

It started as a cup of coffee over the fence but then I started talking about Julian. About what happened last night when we took our separate drugs.

About what happened this morning when we woke up from separate dreams.

And so Brian suggested I climb over the fence and have a beer and smoke a joint and sit in the sunshine on his deck. Which I did.

Digit followed.

Occasionally I could hear the distant ring of Julian's telephone across my garden. But I ignored it. I just smoked and drank and talked and felt the Quaalude easing me into the afternoon.

At least I think it was the Quaalude. Or was it the marijuana?

Or the alcohol?

(Who was it who said looking at one drug through another is like holding up a mirror to a mirror to see what a mirror looks like?)

But no matter. It worked. The combination produced a spectacular effect. It is with me still. I am back at my glass-topped table feeling better than ever. But we will not be here long. I want to get to the café before the afternoon is over. That's why I took Julian's telephone off the receiver and buried it under my pillow—an appropriate resting place while I tell you about Brian. About what I told Brian. About how I sat on his deck and looked back at my life from the outside rather than the inside, seeing it from a new perspective—a separate point of view—as Brian remained scrupulously quiet, for the most part listening rather than talking, offering none of his usual venom toward Julian. Which encouraged me to talk all the more: to ask his opinion and try to figure out why they have never gotten along as neighbors should. As gay men should. *I'm sure it has something to do with the fact they are so much alike—in style if not appearance—since they both work at night. In places which are usually very dark. In fantasies which are usually very real in spite of the fact they deal wholly, very often passionately—maybe even exclusively—with images. Secret Identities. The simple fact that we must all be beautiful—somewhere!*

Brian works at a bar called The Arena. It's just down the street from a place called The Ramrod—which is not very far from The Stud and The Round-up and The Boot Camp and The Hungry Hole. And of course the various baths, more commonly called the "tubs," where gay men go to have sex with each other sometimes. In fact quite often. In tiny rooms with dark halls and loud music that inhabits every sexual transgression. The tubs have names like The Club and The Barracks and The Handball Express—which are the most popular. But there's also a place called The Dungeon, which, according to Brian, is considerably more determined. It has chains attached to walls and rooms padded in leather where homosexuals pretend to beat each other up—usually quite harmlessly. But one time a body was discovered there. It had been dead for several hours and its asshole had been split wide open as if by an ax. Police called it yet another "strand" in the expanding "web" of pathetically brutal homosexual murders in San Francisco—which is a peninsula. It's surrounded on three sides by water and . . . the reality is this: I am very high. My mind is doing crazy things. It is going down dark hallways—through dangerous streets—to far-off places. I look at Brian and see one world—part of Julian's world; but then I look at Brian's garden, at his carefully pampered roses and calla lilies and pansies, and I see something completely different—something which is a part of me.

As if Brian contains us both.

As if Brian is not only the catalyst who first told us about Mexico—but a symbol of everything we went there to escape.

Which was what we didn't like in ourselves.

Do I make any sense? Probably not. As I sat there talking I couldn't help noticing Brian's bathrobe had come undone. I could see his skin was very white and tight. I could see his penis hanging long and darker than the rest of him. He didn't have Julian's kind of muscles but he was firm like a swimmer—and very tall.

With pitch-black hair and a two-day beard that looked good there. It added shadow to the dent in his chin. It made his entire face seem squarer, more boyish—giving depth to his dark eyes and a ghostly contrast to his white skin. And it was particularly effective at night, behind the bar—where the light is sparse and his eyes are groping for signals. He is as at home behind that bar as Julian is at the gym. He wears a loose flannel shirt and jeans so faded and tight that they hide nothing—and in fact give emphasis to the rise between his thighs: the shape that now hangs free. . . .

I had seen it so clearly in everyone's eyes. I had sat there so many times, on so many nights when Julian had to go "out," that I memorized (and in a way idolized) Brian's methodical movement—a motion as precise as dance. He would turn and step and reach and pour and hand and receive and then step on to the next, keeping in touch with the flow, never letting it go. Never wasting a second. Taking three glasses in each hand and then plunging them mouth-open into the water, into the rinse, onto a rack—onto the next—always aware; always set to respond as if cocked like a gun, sensitive to the hand or command that would trigger him into action. And every eye in that place was on him, watching him—desiring him . . . Amazed by his fierce dedication not so much to the performance of his job, but to the artistry of it. As if he were a kind of poet.

As if the tips didn't really matter.

And his bulge made him seem even bigger. The customers couldn't ignore it. They, too, were caught up by the motion—by the stretch of powerful thighs pulling tight against hard denim that was perpetually in action, always defining, giving renewed emphasis to the promise attached to their drinks.

To the purpose attached to their being there.

Whoever hired Brian was very smart. But of course all three bartenders were in one way or another beautiful. What set Brian apart more than anything was the fact that he virtually ignored his tips. The other bartenders had a way of removing the tip so unobtrusively—as they cleaned an ashtray or wiped off the bar—that it was almost an insult. When the customer realized it was gone it was as if he had been deceived. But to Brian that was petty. To him the most important thing was to make the customer feel pampered like his roses. Whenever he gathered his tips he would do it very deliberately—and always with a smile. But usually he would just let the tips gather for drinks on end, sometimes as long as an hour, obviously knowing that many a sly customer would remove a coin rather than add one to the growing pile on the bar. But it didn't matter to Brian—and that's what ultimately made him so endearing: he had a basic trust that in the end he would come out ahead.

And of course he did.

I remember the night I first saw him there. The "night of the sailor," as I call it now. I had gotten so good at following Julian that it seemed almost second nature. I even kept a spare jacket—a jacket that Julian had never seen and therefore wouldn't recognize—in a bottom drawer of my desk. I would put it on quickly, then head out through the garden, over the fence, squeezing between houses and emerging on an upper street which circled around and almost always brought me closely behind Julian. I had a way of hugging the buildings, always prepared to make an about-face or duck quickly inside a doorway if Julian should chance to turn around—which he rarely did. But that night he led me to a seedy section of town called The Tenderloin, where he met a young sailor beneath a neon sign that said PALACE ILLIARDS (the B was burned out), and then they turned quickly down a dark alley, through other dark alleys, finally emerging on a busy thoroughfare popular with the tourists. And then they slowed down. And that's when the sailor kept looking around with eyes that seemed heavier—much older than the rest of him. And then I realized that something else was going on here—that the sailor was not a client. That he probably wasn't even a sailor.

That together they were in on some furtive entanglement that was beyond my understanding—beyond even my curiosity. I had no choice but to halt in my tracks, to look at my reflection in the window of an art gallery and accept the fact that Julian had a friend. A partner in crime! Someone who actually shared the meaning of this part of his life. As if this sailor and I were two parts of the same puzzle, but at opposite ends of Julian's landscape—forbidden by definition to ever touch or fit together.

I don't know how else to explain it. For the first time I felt I had to strike back. My mind was on fire and I didn't realize until I got there that I had headed toward The Arena. I pushed open the door and stepped inside and the place was packed. But Brian, always attentive, noticed me—and came right over to me at the far end of the bar, followed by the eyes of all the men who watched him: who recognized that, probably for the first time, Brian was obviously interested in a customer. Bestowing favor on one. Refusing to accept money for a drink. Looking me right in the eyes and saying with genuine alarm, "You look terrible. You better have a double."

And all night long he kept refilling my glass—usually when it was only half empty—and by midnight I had had time to reconsider the whole thing: to be in a way glad that Julian had a friend of the same species, no matter what it was. No matter where they had gone that night. For the first time since I had met Julian I was enjoying myself without him. Brian's attention became everyone's attention. I began talking to the man sitting next to me, who was eager to find out how I knew Brian. "I don't," I said. "I never saw him before in my life." And in truth I hadn't—at least not like this. Not even over his roses—never so completely in his element. It was as if that bar were a cocoon nurturing him, sustaining him—bringing him again and again toward me, until finally it was closing time and he asked me to stay behind. It wouldn't take long to clean up. We could go have a cup of coffee someplace. And that place turned out to be his apartment.

And the coffee turned out to be wine.

And the only light was a solitary candle that danced between us. I asked him not to turn on the lights, and to keep the curtains open at least a slit, and he didn't have to ask why. It was perfectly dark, no moon or stars. Only the perpetual haze of light that allows no real darkness in a city. I would know when Julian got home—I would see it across the garden—and I was determined to wait: to enter after him. Which was something I had never done before. Usually I was asleep (but sometimes at my typewriter) when Julian slid quietly between our sheets, not really waking me but warming me with his presence—as if pressing himself into my dreams. But tonight would be different, no matter how long I had to stay there with Brian. Except had *isn't the right word. Because suddenly it was transformed into* want. *Because Brian recognized my anxiety and yet said nothing—not a word about Julian. At least not right away. Instead he just kicked off his cowboy boots and propped up his legs and started talking about himself—how he always feels he's "on stage" behind the bar. How all those frantic eyes don't really make him nervous but somehow timid. "They seem to expect something from me," he said. "Something more than I can give them. Something more than anyone can give them."*

Then he reached for a sketch pad and began doodling in the darkness, occasionally sipping his wine and often lapsing completely into silence—but never demanding a response. Making it so easy for me just to be there with him. Always listening attentively to the pauses between his own words, as if they rather than I contained the true intent of his speaking them.

"That place is so weird," he said. "I mean the way it's structured, the way it's designed. The music is purposely loud. The lights are purposely dim. Everything is arranged to accentuate images—to prevent communication. It's as if everyone's on stage," he said, "but people react to it so differently. Some hover in corners, in the deepest of shadows, while others bask in the

light of the pool table—attempting to win not just the game, but the chance to remain in the spotlight. I've seen them all, in varying degrees—in various shapes—and usually it's the younger ones who hang out near the pool table, but not always. Sometimes they're just shy. Sometimes they're just new to the city. Usually it just takes a while to get into it.

"But there's one type I'm always cautious of," Brian said as he doodled, his legs still propped up on the table, the pad on his lap, his feet so big and his toes so thick and square that I wondered how they ever fit into his pointed cowboy boots. "And that's the guy who takes everything so seriously that he always seems to be on stage—even when he's in the shadows. Even when he's on the street or in a supermarket. I see it a lot in this city," he said, "and in that bar," he said, "and I know what I'm talking about.

"I know what it means.

"It means something's wrong," he said, applying his pencil with even more determination to the page. "It means they create their own shape and they thrive too much on it. They are too perfectly arranged—too much in control—and their fantasy is so real that it *is no longer fantasy . . .*

"It is no longer fun.

"Fantasies," he said, "especially sexual fantasies, are meant *to be fun. They are a* logical *extension of our childhood fantasies of wanting to fly or of going to the moon. It makes perfect sense that as we grow older and become more aware of our mortality—of our inability to transcend life and to achieve the fantastic—that we would turn toward our flesh: toward what we have in life as a way of avoiding death while we can. I think that any kind of fantasy, even sexual fantasy—even getting chained to a wall or fucked by a dildo—is healthy as long as it is acknowledged for what it is. And as long as it can be made fun of.*

"And that's what bothers me so much about that guy Julian," he said. "Your friend Julian," he said, sipping his drink, looking me right in the eyes, "just doesn't laugh. He hardly ever

smiles. He takes his muscles far too seriously. He takes his fantasies much too realistically. Even when he's out in your garden it's as if he's performing for the goddamn flowers. He has such a strong sense of his own mortality that he scares me. He scares me for you. It's as if he doesn't want *to get away from death," Brian said.*

"It's as if he'd rather live it," Brian said.

"I bet his father committed suicide," Brian said with such certainty that I suddenly wanted out of there.

I didn't like what he was about to say.

No matter what he was about to say.

But whatever he was about to say didn't come out. He got one good look at my reaction and saw the horror. And knew the truth. And realized he had gone too far—and reached too deep. And suddenly he was apologizing, saying something about the wine getting to his head. Something about how he just wanted to be a friend: how he wanted me to know he was there if I ever needed him, but he didn't mean to scare.

He couldn't presume to know.

Would I like another glass of wine?

He leaped to his feet. He fumbled for my glass. He knocked the sketch pad onto the table. It landed near the candle. It flickered as if to life at the exact moment the lights snapped on across the garden.

In my apartment.

And I saw that it was . . .

Julian!

He had drawn Julian.

It was a caricature—grotesque and distorted, not really lifelike—and yet as real as anything I had ever seen.

As real as what now moved inside my sliding glass doors.

I reached for my jacket. I avoided Brian's eyes. I turned toward the door but I couldn't help turning back—taking a final look at that drawing of a man emaciated, his muscles collapsed, his eyes hollow and terrified, surrounded by leaves that licked like tongues at sores that wouldn't heal.

At wounds that seemed so deep.

Suddenly I had just one thought: to get back to Julian before it was too late. To confess all. To tell him I had been with Brian all night—just waiting for him. Hoping for him.

But before I could reach the door Brian stopped me, actually held me as if to embrace me—as if to kiss me—and then realized that I was trembling.

That there was nothing left to say.

That I wouldn't understand it anyway.

So he let me go without a word and I quickly circled the block, ran madly toward my house, inserted the key, and then made my way directly to the apartment in the rear—hardly pausing to think but knowing somehow that Julian would be angry.

That I should have been there waiting and willing to accept him on his own terms.

Without my silly games.

But when I finally pushed my way inside I was amazed to discover I was wrong. Julian wasn't mad at all. In fact just the opposite. I could tell from his smile and the glow in his eyes that I was suddenly at a premium. That he loved me for not *being there. That he was not about to ask any questions or demand any excuses for whatever choices I had made that night. Instead he just grabbed me and held me and then undressed me right there in the doorway, not even pausing to close the blinds over our sliding glass doors, probably figuring it was the middle of the night and nobody would be out there watching and masturbating as we had the most violent and brutal sex we had ever had.*

The most wonderful and amazing sex we had ever had.

But what does this have to do with last night? Nothing and yet everything! As I looked at Brian's penis hanging long and loose between the folds of his bathrobe, in the sunshine of his deck, I couldn't help considering how little our relationship had changed over the months. I had been to his bar dozens of times, maybe even hundreds of times, all of them when Julian had gone out—all of them ending up in Brian's apartment, in the candlelight—and yet in all that time we had never touched or undressed. I had never even seen his penis. Not until the moment of its unfolding on that deck, when I saw in all its size and splendor that Brian was my way of remaining true to Julian.

A fact so stark I had missed it completely.

Night after night I had followed Julian until I could follow him no more. Down dark streets, through busy intersections—until he entered an apartment or disappeared into a cab or dissolved down a street I dared not travel. Only then would I turn to the bar—to Brian's bar. To Brian's dance of delight over me. To the eyes and faces that followed our every gesture, misinterpreting our friendship, knowing we would go home together—turning even our most casual movements into intimate expressions of love. Turning even my most innocent smile into a blatant betrayal of Julian.

And yet all we ever did was talk. Night after night we lit that candle and sipped our wine and talked about the bar, about the men—about the motion of our universe. About where we had come from and who we were right now, in San Francisco. Even about things like computers, or motorcycles, or even Einstein. Or even God.

Or even the electromagnetic force.

That was the night Brian got really drunk.

He was trying to tell me about an article he had read in Science Digest.

"Basically," he was saying, "it boils down to one scientific truth: opposites attract. Whether you're talking about an atom in your body or an atom in the stars, it's the same electromagnetic force—positive protons attracted to negative electrons—that keeps that atom, and therefore the universe, from flying apart!"

That in itself seemed simple enough. I thought I understood what he was talking about. He was so drunk that he seemed perfectly lucid, almost eloquent. But then his mind wandered and his drink spilled and he started telling me about when he was a kid. About how all the nuns used to hate him and how all the other kids made fun of him because he would get the "atom" of science class mixed up with the "Adam" of religion class.

It occurred to him, he said, even as an adolescent, he said, that they were the same thing—at least until Eve came along.

"Before that, Adam was complete in himself—both positive and negative, male and female—swirling inside the same Adam!"

That's why, according to Brian—who was suddenly speaking very softly, as if revealing a secret—"when the female was pulled from Adam and given its own shape, they had no choice but to attract. Without that they were doomed. Without that they were incomplete—unGodlike.

"It was natural for me to be confused," he said. "But those goddamn nuns beat the shit out of me. They said I was a sinner. They sent notes home to my parents. They made me go to confession. They made me go to communion. They said God was a man, a Father to us all—the Savior of us all—and how dare I imply he was a hermaphrodite!

"Of course I was too young to fight back," he said. "I had never even heard the word before. So I went to the dictionary and looked it up. It said a hermaphrodite is a man who is also a woman. Or a woman who is also a man. 'A combination of diverse elements,' it said—which seemed as good a definition of God as any I had ever heard.

"But of course I was wrong—just as they were wrong.

"I know now," he said, "in my adulthood," he said, "in my moments of awakening with you and this wine," he said, "that God, like love—like knowledge—can have no gender, no sex. If God were man or woman, or even man and woman—positive and *negative, proton and electron—then it would be governed by law: defined in the dictionary: seen in the universe: explained by* Science Digest.

"God cannot be any of this or else we would understand it!" he shouted. "We would bring it down to our *level. It would have* equal *footing. Maybe even lesser footing. It would not be God. . . .*

"Don't you see?" Brian cried out. "God has to be something more subtle than particles and forces, crosses and communions. If anything God has to be the basic particle, the ether that contains all*—that cannot be measured by electromagnetism or gravity or the speed of light. Or the shape of genitals!*

"To hell with the electromagnetic force!" he said. "Fuck Science Digest*!" he said. "Let me propose a toast to you!" he said.*

"And to me!" he said.

"And to likes attracting!

"And to opposites repelling!

"And to laws collapsing!

"And to the universe embracing us all*!"*

He was very drunk. He had to lean forward and examine the table very carefully before he placed his drink on it. And then he burped. And then he looked out at the shadows and up at the moon. And then back at me. And then he finally said, as if it followed very logically, as if there had been no interruption to his thought process whatsoever: "When you first got back from Mexico I was a little worried. You seemed so happy in your Garden of Eden. I thought you would never come back to me again. A hundred times a night I would look at your spot at the end of the bar and imagine you sitting there, your head so low, your shoulders so slumped: your eyes so desperate for the kind of contact that would take you up and out of yourself—and back to me. . . .

"At last I can say it," he said. "At last I have realized it," he said. "I was using you. I am *using you—using your sadness, using even your despair to attract you night after night like some animal into . . . my lair!" he shrieked, giggling at the rhyme.*

Recognizing the intent.

"That is my *fantasy," he said. "The fantasy of touching your mind and then watching your body with Julian. I think I delight in the fact that you always go back to him. I think I love you for never talking about him—for holding him so sacred—for allowing me to take what little you give me while letting me know it is more than I have ever had before.*

"What I'm trying to say is thank you," he said. "Thank you for the mystery. Thank you for your pain.

"Thank you for my *pain.*

"Boy am I drunk," he said. "Too drunk to cry," he said. "How about another toast?" he laughed. "And this time I mean it," he said. "This time I wish to propose a toast To Mystery . . .

"To what I can't explain.

"To what I know is true!"

And now I have put it into perspective for you. Now you can see how different it was today in the daylight, in the shadow of Brian's sex—without the candle or the moonlight or the certain expectation of Julian. . . .

He was gone and I had accepted it. I tried to explain that to Brian. I looked at his penis and remembered the bar and tried to tell him that on some level I, too, had been using him—my genuine attraction to him—to somehow get at Julian. To make Julian think I'm something that fulfills his expectations. But last night I could deceive Julian no longer . . .

Last night it had come to a head.

It was just after dark when I took a Quaalude and Julian smoked some angel dust.

I had told Brian before—as I had told Julian before—how much I hated angel dust. But Julian wouldn't listen to me. His telephone hadn't rung and it was well into the evening and he was in one of his moods. He was pacing the floor. Even Digit the cat kept clear of him. So when he decided to smoke the angel dust I couldn't take it anymore. I told him again how it was an animal tranquilizer, that it numbed him beyond recognition—that it made him cold and distant and at times even terrifying. "You should see yourself when you take that stuff," I said. "Your neck puffs out. Your eyes diminish into two little dots that all but disappear. Your body turns blue and you look grotesque," I said. "You look dead," I said.

But instead of saying a word he just reached into his front pocket and pulled out a handful of Quaaludes, knowing my weakness, slamming them onto the corner of my desk, looking me right in the eyes and then proceeding to roll himself a joint—deliberately lacing it with an almost lethal amount of the dazzling white powder that looked so pure and inviting, so innocent and enchanting, and yet certainly from no angel.

Certainly from no God.

"It was awful," I told Brian. "I started to panic. I started saying all kinds of things I knew I would regret later. I didn't mean to tell him about us—that's not what I intended to do—it's just that I couldn't help myself when he brought the joint to his lips. When I saw him reach for the matches and I knew this was my last chance. I thought maybe by explaining about you, about our 'affair of the mind'—about all the nights I had sat at your bar or sipped near your candle but waited for him, always for him—that I might snap him out of it. That I might talk him back *to me!"*

At that moment Brian shifted nervously in his seat. I could tell he didn't really want to hear it. Or was it that he already knew it? He crossed and then uncrossed his legs. He adjusted his robe as if trying to hide something—as if for the first time he were feeling naked.

But it was too late for me to stop now.

"Do you know what I'm talking about?" I said. "But of course you don't! I haven't even told you about the sailor Julian meets in front of a poolhall every Thursday night. Or the old man

Julian put to bed like a child one night. Or the cunt I see Julian shaving again and again in my mind every night. In my mirrors every night!

"There were so many nights," I said, "and I threw them all at Julian—as fast as I could, as hard as I could. One right after another, as if they were evidence. As if they were a conviction. But still he didn't say anything—not a goddamn syllable. Not even when I screamed at him, shed tears for him. He just looked at me from so far away, already cold and blue, as if I had deceived him—as if I *were the cunt.*

"As if I were the slut!

"I had no choice but to take that Quaalude," I told Brian. "If for no other reason than to get away from Julian. To protect myself from the way he finally struck a match and inhaled so deeply, and then held it so long—not wanting to waste it.

"Not wanting to lose a breath of it.

"Doing it to himself as if to me.

"Leaning so far back into his chair, and into himself, that I thought he would never come out. I thought he would never speak up.

"But he did," I said. "Finally he did, and what he had to say came from very far away—as if through a tunnel. As if from the center of the earth. It was a cry, not a word—and it was so heavy and so damp and so dark and so true that I'm not even sure I heard it. I'm not even sure I remember it. My Quaalude was coming on quickly. I was getting high much faster than usual. Probably because my blood was rushing so fast. Probably because as I look at it now everything seems so different from last night.

"I don't know where I am anymore.

"I don't know what really happened anymore.

"My God, Brian, who am I? What the fuck am I telling you? Do you have any idea how really dark it is in here without Julian?

"Without hope!"

Suddenly I was lost. Suddenly I looked up at Brian as if

from the wrong end of a telescope and remembered something about a journal. Or a journey. Or . . .

A dream—that was it! Now I remember. A dream about tears. A dream about all my worst fears coming true. There were two of us in bed and one of us was meant to be murdered. The other was a witness, an object of circumstance. Everything was white—the only color. And blue—the only feeling. At first I thought it was a hospital but then the walls turned to clouds and the light arrived so quickly—like a burst of sun behind the morning fog that tumbles down my hillside. And then a third man entered. He was wearing a uniform and yet he was naked, as if the uniform were his shape—his flesh. He sifted through the clouds and pointed the gun and shot the other man with tears. I knew they were tears because they were so soft. Because they seemed to hurt so much. *And then he turned the gun toward me and stepped closer and aimed it very carefully, very deliberately at my head. I looked up and I could see him standing directly above me and for a moment I thought he was a sailor. And for a moment I thought he was a postman. And for a moment I was certain he was a cab driver. But it didn't really matter because at that moment he pulled the trigger and I heard the noise and I saw the explosion and I woke up screaming.*

Julian was beside me dreaming.

He told me about it in the morning.

He said he dreamed he had heard a scream. It was the middle of the night. He had just walked into a room. He saw me lying on a bed, next to a body, and a gun was pointing at my head. And a man was pulling the trigger. And what came out was not tears—it was come, he said. It was sperm, he said. It splashed in my eyes and entered my mouth and covered my flesh and ate me alive, he said.

And ate me inside, he said.

And then I woke up. This time I really woke up. Julian was beside me on the bed. He wasn't speaking a word. He wasn't dreaming a thing. It was as if he were still high on angel dust. He was so moody and silent as he reached for a cigarette, obviously remembering what I had said last night. Probably deciding at that moment to take his shower and pack a bag and leave me behind with his telephone.

And leave me alone with his Quaaludes . . .

I tried to explain it to Brian on the deck today. I tried to tell him how little was said this morning—and yet how much I had heard in the silence. "Who was it who said reality is the price we pay for dreams?" I asked him. "Who was it who said pain is the only food of thought—since pleasure ends in itself?" I admitted the Quaalude or maybe the joint was still making me high. That it was getting awfully hot out there. That I was maybe saying too much and getting really thirsty and maybe we better have another beer. So he got up and headed through the sliding glass door and came back out with a Budweiser and a Michelob and gave me my choice. And then he turned his chair around and faced me and sat down and slid off his robe and allowed the sun to hit his back. And allowed his penis to hang longer and thicker and with a great deal more purpose than before. It was as if the weight of my message were finally registering with him—actually exciting him. I could see what he intended to do. I could see everything rising so clearly in front of me. I looked at him and I saw Julian and I knew that nothing was over between us; that nothing would be over between Julian and me until one of us had been devoured by his drug . . .

Or until one of us had been murdered in his dreams!

"Stop it!" I shouted at Brian, suddenly losing control. "Do you know what the fuck it's doing to me?" I said, reaching out and taking it in my hand and squeezing it. "Look at yourself!" I shrieked, actually yanking it, trying to hurt it, unable to believe it *was so much bigger than I had imagined—so much bigger than anyone had imagined could hide inside that bulge beneath blue denim.*

"What a joke!" I said. "Our whole relationship, our entire 'affair of the mind'—what chance does it stand against that*?*

"How could anybody ever resist that*?*

"No wonder they love you!" I said. "No wonder they watch you and wait for you and hope for you and get drunk on you. And would kill for you," I said, "if only they could see you as I do . . .

"If only they could know your reality is beyond even their wildest fantasies!

"But not me," I said. "I no longer want any part of you. Not even this part of you. Julian was right this morning when he said you and I are the madmen—the doodlers and dreamers! The ones to be watched and the ones to be afraid of!

"And this proves it," I said, trying to push him away. Knowing I had to.

Knowing I couldn't.

"Did Julian ever deceive me? No! Did he ever try to hide his angel dust? No! Did he ever lie to me or follow me or tell me he was something he wasn't? No! No! No! Not once did he even pretend to know the meaning of God or the universe or the electromagnetic field of love!

"But he did show me one thing," I told Brian—except suddenly I couldn't remember it. Suddenly it was so important that it was lost. I thought maybe it had something to do with Mexico but I wasn't sure. Brian was too close, too big, too real—and too good to be true. I looked in his eyes and I squeezed with my hand and I tried to explain but . . . but all I could remember was something about a journal. Or a journey. Or a dream. Or . . .

A Quaalude—that was it! Now I remember. I had taken a Quaalude. We had sat on his deck. He had opened his robe. I had reached for the truth. And now I am back.

I have never been gone.
You are all I have left.
And God help me now!

M*exico. It's time now to tell you about Mexico. I have been putting it off too long. It's late afternoon and the fog is waiting to return. It's hovering up the hillside, threatening to descend with the night. I'm outdoors now, at a café—in a jacket that Julian has never seen—sitting and writing and sipping a double espresso, hoping it will help me to see things more clearly: knowing that Quaalude nearly knocked me out—distorted everything. But I'm not going to apologize. Not to you and not to Brian and not to anyone. I don't even know who you are. Why you could be anybody—anywhere in my future. Somebody I know or somebody I've yet to meet. Or maybe even a stranger—maybe a thief who will steal this notebook when I go inside for another double espresso. Only one thing is certain: the present. The present and the presence of the fog. The past and this pen in my hand. And the crashing waves. And the diminishing light. And the power of bringing purpose into perspective!*

Yes, I'm still a little high. But there's no way to stop it now. There are people all around me—witnesses to my crime. People smoking or sipping or talking or laughing or reading at tiny tables. In open air. Near city streets separated only by a border of glass—a fence you can see through. The outside is an extension of the inside—visibly, through plants and flowers surrounding that glass, growing in planters on either side of it, arranged not so much to give an illusion but to create a reality. And to protect us from the cold, which eventually will descend with the fog. . . .

The building itself is on a corner and has a view of intersecting streets. I can lean back against it as I sit here in the open. It is made almost entirely of glass with a tin roof that is magical when the rains arrive. The water literally tap-dances on that roof as the wind howls and beads of water race their way in every direction across the glass. No matter where you sit in the L-shaped room you can see outside in at least two directions. And from certain vantage points you can actually see through glass to see through glass to see back inside. But during a heavy storm the windows get steamed and the water slams hard and the shapes outside seem distorted as they struggle with umbrellas or overcoats, finally shaking off the water and stepping inside and becoming instantly aroused, as if physically stimulated by the enormous scent of steaming espresso which is especially keen on a wet day.

But I like to sit outside. Especially on a day like today, when the wind is brisk but there's still some sun and some hope the fog will not descend too quickly. It is important for me to place you here: to actually seat you at my table and share my espresso and invite you into my intimacy—an intimacy that can exist only in a crowd of strangers. For some reason I feel more relaxed here, on neutral territory, than I did in my apartment. Suddenly it is easier for me to just "be" with you—to ease you onto this page and tell you truly that you are a part *of what is going on. Not an observer, but a character who must be taken into account—as real as the man sitting across from me. He's just yards away, sipping coffee and reading sheet music and sometimes looking off at the fog—at the diminishing brightness—as if he, too, is in another time, with another person. He is tall and dark with a black beard and hands that belong on a motorcycle, not sheet music. I have seen him several times on the street and we recognize each other now and we nod and smile and seem to say hi, although we've never actually spoken a word. I've never actually heard his voice. And yet he is someone who, in a very peculiar way, is a real force in my life. Whenever I see him coming down the street I invariably feel my muscles tightening and my heart pounding and my mind struggling for the right tone—the right depth, the right pitch—to utter that one word I know I will never say: "Hi." And* when he has gone by I force myself not to look back, not to see if he is looking back—for if he is, and if I do, then the fantasy is over and the reality begins and that is why I do not approach him even now: because I am here with you. Because this moment belongs to us, not him, and it feels so good to be on this page with you. It's as if I am with an old friend. I thought we would never get away from Brian. At least not without submitting to him—without abandoning all hope of ever returning to Julian! But the truth is, I think, that Brian loves me; is willing to wait for me—is waiting in fact to gather me like he gathers his tips: with the certain knowledge that in the end he will come out ahead.

And of course he . . .

(The bearded man is getting up now. He's gathering his music and draining the last of his coffee now. He's stepping forth and squeezing between tables now. And heading past me now. As I write these words to you now. And . . . And . . .)

My handwriting is a mess. I admit it gets worse as I move along. I'll have to pay more attention to what I'm doing. It's just that I'm not used to pens. I've become so electrified by typewriters that keep me on a straight line, an even keel, that it is hard for me to get back to a basic sense of touch. Of me applying the pressure to this page, actually pressing myself into it—rather than having some invention doing it for me . . . for you.

Touch—that was the keynote of our entire trip. Which lasted two weeks, not one—at Julian's suggestion. He said if we're going that far then we may as well make something of it. He said we should have new swim suits, and new shorts—and snorkels and masks and fins. And one of those Polaroid cameras, the kind that produces a photo in sixty seconds. "Instant past!" he laughed when he gave it to me. "We won't have to wait to get home to have our memories."

It was a golden period—that part of Mexico that began here in San Francisco. Those days when we shopped and planned and packed as if for some great adventure. That goofy photo we had *someone else take at the ticket counter as we stood with our suitcases—already wearing snorkels and masks beneath a huge sign that said* AEROMEXICO. *All those frantic moments that led to that one moment of departure—that soaring high over the skies of San Francisco—were magical. They had already made our trip worthwhile. What I didn't expect was the feeling I had when we finally left the ground—when I felt Julian's arm beside me and the city below me and the thrust inside me—and I knew there was no turning back.*

And I knew this must be some dream.

The only dark aspect of our departure was the mescaline. Two tiny capsules containing chemicals that could take us higher than any plane—beyond any border. Julian insisted we hide them amid the vitamins. "They'll be looking for marijuana," he said. "They'll never expect this stuff." I tried to talk him out of it—to convince him that we didn't need any drugs, not this time—but he wouldn't hear of it. He was certain they wouldn't find it. He couldn't understand or maybe just wouldn't accept the fact that I wanted to leave all *of the city behind me.*

It was important, you see, that everything go according to plan. It was important for me to find that restaurant in Yelapa precisely as I had imagined it. Already I could see the candlelight and taste the lobster and know that some great truth was about to be imposed on us. I expected it to arrive like a bolt of lightning, or a flicker of flame—but always the same: with an immense weight attached to it. Almost a death attached to it, as if once it arrived there would be no escape.

As if we were doomed to be happy.

But first there was Puerto Vallarta, where we would spend several days before we took the boat to Yelapa. Where we landed as planned and made our way through customs without incident—as Julian predicted. We changed our dollars into pesos and then checked into a hotel and quickly changed into our shorts and headed directly to the seashore to get an immediate start on that deep, rich tan that would last long after we returned to San Francisco. But it didn't take us long to realize that Puerto Vallarta was also a city, at least by Mexican standards, which meant it was more like a large small town that thrived almost entirely on the tourists. All the streets were cobblestone and all the hotels were built around courtyards and the beach was lined with restaurants and shops and high-rises and even discos that played very loud American music until the early hours of the morning. And then there was Carlos O'Brian's, where all the oiled tourists sat in the late afternoon and tempted each other with stares and even winks as they sipped tequila and ordered hors d'oeuvres and kept applying lotion as if it were emotion to their tans. And the local cinema was named after Elizabeth Taylor and one of the bars was named after Richard Burton and heaven knows how many people mentioned the fact that the movie Night of the Iguana *was filmed just down the coast, just south of town—and yet we loved it. Loved all of it. The whole tourist bit! We shopped every morning and sunned every afternoon and drank every evening and when somebody asked if we were brothers Julian just laughed and said, "Yeah, in a way we are." And at night we did everything except go to the discos. That's because they wouldn't admit men who weren't accompanied by women. That's because there were so many Mexican men hovering outside, trying to get inside to put the make on American women and so they had to keep them out somehow. But we had no interest in American women, or even Mexican women. Or even Mexican or American men. We were happy just to have some exotic seafood at a beachside restaurant and then to head to some quieter bar where we could brush legs and touch arms and compare tans. And then we would go back to our hotel and make love beneath that monstrous ceiling fan which was always in motion, accompanied by the perpetual sound of immense waves crashing and kissing the seashore just off our balcony—as if the ocean itself were inhabiting our sex. As if nature herself were nodding approval!*

How it hurts for me to go back to that time. I can actually feel the ache of wanting to return there again. Those opening days were like the first act of a play—dazzling in the display of sets and thoughts that unfolded so quickly, with such certainty, as if they had a purpose. As if every look we exchanged was destined to deepen—to reveal an even greater truth as time went on. How drab this café seems next to all that. Even on a sunny day you can sense a kind of despair here—a gloom that can hover like fog over the city. So many people I see around me have long hair and no qualms about smoking dope out in the open. They hang out for hours and write in their journals or draw in their sketch pads or play on their guitars and talk about visions but they never seem to be in a hurry to get anywhere. Somebody wrote in the bathroom, "The road to success is always under construction."

But the road to Yelapa just didn't exist. The jungle was too full of snakes and scorpions and iguanas and a landscape so lush, so thick and dense that it wasn't worth the expense of hacking out a highway to that tiny village of our dreams. But there was one boat a day, every day, which left Puerto Vallarta in the morning and returned late in the afternoon and it was always packed with tourists who danced and drank on board. There was a live band with Latin music and a full bar with exotic drinks served in coconut shells or pineapple rinds as the boat chugged its steady course south and parallel to land. And when it was announced that one couple was celebrating their fortieth wedding anniversary everybody clapped. And when it was announced that another couple was on their honeymoon everybody hooted and applauded. And as the day got hotter the music got louder. And the drinks disappeared faster. And after three rum pineapples in the hot sun I told Julian I wanted them to announce us, *to acknowledge* our *rela-*

tionship, and that I was going to walk over and tip the bandleader to do just that. At first Julian laughed but then he saw I was serious and then he saw me digging into my pocket and heading across the dance floor and I'm not sure what happened next. I don't know what made me turn back to look at him. I just know that what I saw made me think of myself—a child afraid. A boy on a horse. A moment so big that Julian was unable to move in any direction. He couldn't accept and he couldn't retreat. The horror was so obvious and his panic so real that I reacted instinctively. I reached for the camera around my neck. I didn't even bother to focus. I just aimed it at Julian and pressed the shutter and saw the photo pop out. And heard the announcement that Yelapa was coming into sight.

Suddenly there was confusion. People scrambled for a view. The photo was knocked from my hand before it had time to develop. I retrieved it quickly and buttoned it into my shirt pocket and knew it would have to remain there until the time was right. Until the feeling was right. But for the moment the situation was resolved for us. In the excitement there was too much to do. We had to gather our baggage and wait our turn to board one of the smaller boats that circled our larger craft, waiting to carry passengers to shore. Not to mention mail and supplies for the villagers whose very lives orbited our arrival. But Julian went first and as I was handing him down our baggage somebody was saying "No more—full up!" And then the boat was pushed toward shore and another was pulling up and suddenly I went crazy. I was blinded as if by rage. I couldn't accept the fact that we would be separated. I couldn't allow the idea of even five minutes away from him. I yanked off the camera and tossed it at Julian and dove mindlessly into the water, passionately into the water, swimming alongside. Refusing to let him out of my sight. Knowing this was the one moment that belonged to both of us. Determined this was the one start we were going to make together.

If this is the beginning of act two, I remember telling myself, then damn it, I'm *going to be in control.*

From now on I wouldn't even let him take a shower alone.

And that is the real beginning of this story—of that time and magic that would carry me through even the darkest moments of our return to San Francisco. I don't know how many times I've sat in this café, or at Brian's bar, and remembered the feeling of my feet touching shore—as if at last arriving in a foreign country. (As if Puerto Vallarta had been part of America.) Instantly we were surrounded by a flurry of natives urging us to eat in this restaurant, or to stop by that shop, or to rent a room in their house, but we had already decided to spend our first night on the beach. That's why we had brought our sleeping bags—or rather, a *sleeping bag. We had the whole thing figured out. We knew exactly what we were doing. We wasted no time making our way toward one end of the horseshoe beach, to the fringe of all the tourists, and then etching out a place in the sand. Forming contours with a purpose. As if building a nest. Spreading out towels and opening up the sleeping bag and unpacking our snorkeling gear and then ordering a beer from one of the vendors passing by. The beach was crowded with people from the boat, foreigners with their lotion, the commotion of Mexicans marching among them—mainly children selling shirts and blouses their mothers had embroidered, or beers and Cokes their fathers kept cold with the daily supply of ice now being unloaded; or melons, or pineapples, or pastries—and still all the outdoor restaurants were crowded. And the shops were busy. And the ocean was alive with laughter. And the hills around us were dotted with thatched rooftops and splashes of color as if bright towels were hanging on lines. And yet the overwhelming color was blue—blue of sky and water. Even blue where sky met land. The vegetation so lush, so dark and heavy on the hillsides surrounding the inlet, sweeping toward the beach, that even the greens seemed blue. Even the leaves seemed true to a world at one with the heavens.*

And then it happened. The boat that had brought us here sounded out like some mournful whale. Within a matter of minutes the center of the beach was clustered with passengers clutching their newly bought treasures, boarding the smaller boats that would take them to the larger boat that would return them to Puerto Vallarta in time for late-afternoon cocktails at Carlos O'Brian's. Already the natives were folding chairs and taking down tables and closing their shops. Even before the boat lifted anchor the beach was all but deserted, void of everything but a handful of tourists who had remained behind to watch the boat—their only connection with the outside world—receding out of the inlet. Toward the ocean. Around the last bend of land as the band on board suddenly struck up music, followed by shrieks and laughter and a steady clapping of hands that gradually diminished with distance, as if into whisper . . .

As if it were still there—and yet not there.

And then Julian and I went about our business. There were a number of things to do before dark. The first item was to check out the hotel on the beach, the only building with its own generator—and therefore electricity. And therefore hot water. Not that we needed the luxury, but we loved the way it was situated, in an arc surrounding the water, each of twenty "rooms" a tiny hut unto itself—with a grass roof and bamboo blinds and a mosquito net over the bed, as if shrouding it in mystery. I knew from Brian's description that this was the place to stay, right here on the beach rather than up the hill in the village, and I couldn't believe it when the man said we were very lucky—that number twenty would be vacant tomorrow. Number twenty was the one farthest up the beach, closest to where the hill suddenly climbed very steeply, built on a slight incline just a few yards above lapping waves—undoubtedly the most isolated "room" of the hotel.

The one most distant from the main building which housed an office and the restaurant and the only mechanical device in Yelapa: the generator. Maker of light and noise.

It was too good to be true. Right away Julian gave him a deposit—and a bit of something extra for his kindness. "For your trouble." Julian was very smart. Immediately the man smiled beneath his mustache. He shook both of both our hands and assured us we could check in anytime after the boat arrived. That, he didn't have to say, was the only timepiece on which Yelapa depended.

So we spent the rest of the day walking the dirt paths and scouting the village and planning a day when we would hike to the waterfall. And then locating the restaurant Brian had told us about, heading there like pilgrims to a shrine—believers with a motive. We expected it to be just another drab building in the daylight, and it was. But at night we knew the candles would transform it, deepen it—extend it into shadows, flickers, ghosts, images of what we would make it. Shapes of what it could be.

Yes, we were greedy. We wanted to gobble each other up. Whenever we encountered someone on the paths, be it tourist or Mexican, we were always polite but never overly enthusiastic—immediately exchanging smiles and small greetings but not real conversation. Nothing that would take away from us.

Nothing that would dispel our magic.

Everything went as if according to some vision. Even the donkeyshit seemed a part of some plan. Even the women washing clothes in a stream, worlds away from the tourists who photographed them, could offer no contradictions. That night we purposely did not go to any restaurant. We kept quietly to ourselves and bought some candles and some cheese and a bottle of wine. And some fruit which we carefully peeled just before sunset—just as the sky turned red and the sun actually bled its way into the Pacific. If only some small thing had gone wrong, some slight imperfection, then I might have been able to sleep. But how could I *with Julian so close? And the stars so naked? And the ocean so soothing—oozing as if inside me? We lay locked inside our sleeping bag as if into a mutual decision: a precision that would be maintained at all costs, like the well-oiled machine at the other end of that beach—the generator which sounded out in the distance, as if from another country, as a symbol of everything we had come here to escape: the hum of humanity. The echo of uncertainty. The knowledge that nothing lasts forever . . .*

But the photograph. I had forgotten it completely! It was as if that moment had never happened—had never been recorded. It must still be in my shirt pocket, in the pile of dirty clothes which now served as our mattress, distorted by salt water and dried by the sun and now crumpled by our weight. And certainly out of focus. And yet it wouldn't be until after we had returned to San Francisco—until it had gone through another soaking, this time in a machine—that I would again remember it. Discover it. Accept it as evidence—proof that there was a death implicit in every new breath of Julian.

What I didn't figure on were the women. The two women who arrived one day as we did—with sleeping bags and knapsacks and a camera that was complete in itself. It was the same day we had hiked to the waterfall, returning as if from a session of prayer in time to watch the boat depart. We had seen it arrive hours ago, from atop the precipice which contained the pool that swelled and constantly spilled downward, surging over rocks and crashing with incredible thunder hundreds of feet in the jungle below. It had taken us an hour to climb, proceeding very cautiously, keeping within each other's grasp and yet on separate ground—admitting it was foolish, that if something should happen no one else was around. But knowing the privacy was worth it.

Accepting the danger as ours.

But how could we figure on the women? They hadn't even arrived yet. And nobody else had offered any competition. The single men certainly had no interest in us. And the single women were too busy battling the single men. And the couples were completely oblivious. And the Mexicans were in another world. And so that left Julian and me free to explore not just outwardly, but inwardly—and passionately. Making love night after night in number twenty, after long walks on the beach; after lingering glances over lobster—inside a mosquito net that seemed to bind us as if in flesh, as the tide outside our door continually lapped and swelled, rose and fell for days without end or beginning. Just one perpetual motion. An extension of the ocean inside us. As if we, too, were at the hands of a moon that grew brighter and holier every hour, tugging harder and heavier every night; not just knowing, but feeling *it would be full by next Friday—the night we would take the mescaline.*

The eve of our last full day in Yelapa.

The height of all possible expectation!

The boat arrived as a speck of white in the distance. We could see it all the way up the coast, at least a half-hour away—long before it would be seen by the people in the village far below us. Or by the people on the beach below them. And yet they knew, as they always knew by the sun, that it was almost here. We watched them scurrying like ants down the paths, onto the shore, tugging on donkeys and burros, unloading their baskets and bottles. Or setting up tables. Or opening up canopies. Or readying their boats. But our view was so spectacular, and that pool on the precipice so inviting—so gently overflowing—that we quickly abandoned the distractions on the beach. And the distant echo of the waterfall crashing below. There was something about being right where we were—so far away from the ocean, so high up the mountain—that it held us down to earth. As if gravity itself had suddenly won out: overcome the moon. Summoned us inward. Motioned us deeper. As if into a scent. As if into a Garden of Eden. . . .

That soil was so fertile; that water so clear as it spiraled out of the jungle, downward toward us—into ripples that allowed us to create, among orchids which grew in the wild—that we couldn't help ourselves. We finally took off all our clothes. We literally tore into that pool, ripping as if it were flesh, cutting as if we were knives, meeting underwater and emerging together as if free of Original Sin. That's really the only way to explain the . . . baptism which occurred. As if all that went before had instantly been forgotten. As if all that lay ahead had already been forgiven. Even the leather and steel.

Even the beckoning moon. . . .

Even from a distance we knew something was up. As soon as we reached the beach we realized there were too many people. Usually they retreated into huts or shadows immediately after the boat departed, but today even some Mexicans had hung around to attend to the possibilities. Not that it was anything like when the boat was here, but still too many people for that time of day—and too many men. Right away Julian noticed it. And pointed to those two women at the center of it.

"Not necessarily the cause," he joked. "But certainly the catalyst."

Julian had an instinct for such things. Maybe even a fascination. He led us directly into the thick of it. One of them was tall and blond—slender like a model—with tiny tits that orbited independently as she reached to retrieve a racquet. The other was much shorter and shapelier, with darker hair, fuller hips, and two lips that attended her Chapstick. Separately they were very beautiful—but together they were dazzling, as if the contrast were a part of some concept; as if their friendship implied a conceit. No wonder all eyes on the beach seemed to follow them, play badminton with them. Even the other women had no choice but to acknowledge a certain enchantment. The natural way those two women seemed to enjoy each other as they related to the people around them: not really dismissing any of the men, but making sure to keep them all at a certain . . . distance. Accepting no invitations. Making no obvious romantic responses. Finally gathering their belongings and avoiding all glances as they strolled casually into number nineteen . . .

The cabin right next to ours.

It was Julian who said they were lesbian. Immediately I exploded into laughter. It was that same night—at the restaurant. The two women were sitting only tables away. For a moment I thought they had heard us. The blond one looked directly my way with eyes that burned like candles. (Later she would tell me she hadn't heard it—but felt it. Sensed *that we were talking about them.) "I mean it," Julian whispered. "They're just too damn together to be anything but queer."*

But he was wrong. Later we learned the truth. After we had avoided them for two days one of them knocked on our door. The dark one. It was late afternoon. I could feel all eyes on the beach looking our way. Julian was still napping naked on the bed behind me. I had just gotten out of the shower and had a wet towel wrapped around my waist.

"Hi!" she said right away, extending her hand. "My name's Dianne. My friend Pamela and I would like to take you two guys out to dinner tonight. Whaddya say?"

What do *you say?*

Suddenly I was in a spotlight.

The entire beach must have guessed what she was doing.

We had to have a pretty goddamn good excuse to not go out with them.

I remember reaching everywhere for an answer.

"Sure," I finally said. "Why not? What time are you guys gonna pick us up?"

She loved it. I could tell she loved it.

She burst into laughter.

"Don't tell me you two have watches!" she said.

Then she pointed to the distant shoreline—to where the last piece of land jutted sharply out into the ocean. "Wait till that's completely in shadow," she said. "Then c'mon over to number nineteen. We'll have a round of drinks before we head up the hill to the restaurant."

"All right," I said.

"Great!" she said.

"Should be fun," I lied.

"Should be more than that," she said, indicating my towel. Winking as she finally turned away.

Then:

"Say, what's your name? You do have a name, don't you?"

"Yes," I said. "It's Robert."

"And your friend?"

I remember concentrating really hard on my smile.

"Julian," I said. "His name is Julian."

It's getting really cold. Soon it will be dark. All but a few of us have moved inside. The fog is closer than ever. I keep asking myself why I'm staying here—why I'm going back there. Did those two women really come to mean so much to us in that short expanse of a week? In that chemistry which created new definitions—new ways of dealing with time? Like something out of Einstein. Traveling so fast that you're actually slowing down—staying young. I remember one night Brian and I had had a long talk about it. About how if a man could travel at nearly the speed of light, say in a spaceship to a distant planet nine light-years away, and then turn around and come back, he would be at most six hours older. But everyone on Earth would be a full eighteen years older.

"It's true!" Brian had said. "The possibility of time travel in empty space was one of Einstein's first discoveries. One of the principal conclusions of Special Relativity.

"Let me make it simpler," he said. "Remember Magellan—the first time traveler? Remember how the survivors of his

around-the-world voyage of 1519–22 arrived home and found they had somehow 'lost' a day? Can you imagine their confusion—their bewilderment? They checked their logs and found them to be meticulous. Every day had *been accounted for. And yet they had somehow* missed *a day. What a shock it was to them then. . . .*

"What a shock it is to us now—the understanding we can have of the Universe!"

One of them was a hostess; the other a barmaid. They both worked at a bar-restaurant called The St. George, in St. Louis. It was a very "singles" place, they said. "Heavy cruisy."

They laughed a lot. They touched their faces a lot. They reached out to us a lot.

Everybody watched.

Everybody saw them order another round of margaritas.

Suddenly time took on new meaning. Immediately Julian took on new dimension. How happy he was for the women's presence. How he loved the idea of the four of us being together, as if in a spaceship. Not that he was disenchanted with the thought of just the two of us—but with four it was somehow easier. And with women it was somehow more special—the feeling we could have for each other.

The way Julian and I could be so separate across that table—and yet closer than ever before.

"You must realize my wink at you today was just a joke," Dianne said to me at one point—completely out of context. "I have absolutely no intention of ever undressing you, Robert."

There was something about the way she pronounced my name that scared me. As hard as I tried, I just couldn't get the feeling she was lying. . . .

Julian looked at me from across the table.

"Listen," Pamela said very seriously, as if that were her cue. "There's something we better tell you guys. Dianne and I talked

about it earlier today. We decided if we really liked you we would be honest. And we do. And so we are.

"And so this is it:

"We're here to have a good time," she said. "Period," she said. "Nothing too heavy and nothing artificial."

"What Pam means," Dianne interrupted, "is that we're just plain tired of the singles scene. We work in it. We live in it. . . ."

"It seems to follow us everywhere we go," said Pam, "as if it's part of being a woman under twenty-five."

"And living in St. Louis."

"And so when we bought our tickets to Mexico we decided to make a rule: no men. Maybe that sounds foolish, but—well, that's just the way we decided to have it."

"Needed *to have it," said Dianne. "Just to relax. Just to be real."*

"And then you two guys came along," Pam said. "We watched the way you kept snorkeling together, keeping to yourselves—the only men allowing us to be alone without our being rude."

"That's the problem," said Dianne. "We just hate to act as if we're . . . above other people."

"And so right away we considered two possibilities," said Pam. "Either you're gay, or else you're just like us. Just wanting *to be alone."*

"Or else both," said Dianne.

"But does it matter?" said Pam.

"We're here to have fun, *" said Dianne.*

"Don't you see?" said Pam. "We can be more alone by being together. Whoever you are, and whoever we are—we can find out!"

"Yeah," said Dianne, throwing me a wink. "Whaddya say?"

It happened so fast. In a way I felt robbed. As if a part of Julian had suddenly been taken away from me. Had actually been extracted from me. And yet when I saw the wonder in Julian's eyes—the magic that danced like candlelight across his face—I was quickly overwhelmed by a feeling of . . . generosity! As if some unspoken prayer had been answered. As if for the first time in his life Julian had been accepted flat out—not for his body. Not for the promise of his flesh. But for whoever he *was. Whatever he decided to* be *with these two women.*

Can you understand the magnitude of such an event in Julian's life?

Can you understand the gratitude in my comprehension of it?

Suddenly things were on a level I couldn't possibly have foreseen in San Francisco.

How could *I have expected this much from Julian?*

And yet there it was: in all of us. In the one *of us. Hiking again to the waterfall. Renting donkeys one day for an outing. Playing badminton together on the beach. Splashing and laughing and snorkeling and at one point even singing. Actually setting up a kind of "camp"—our spot on the sand. Joining sleeping bags and bringing out pillows, Polaroids, a Frisbee, their transistor radio, a deck of cards—days of sunshine and laughter! Of taking simultaneous photos that transpired in exactly sixty seconds—as if we had willed them into perspective.*

As if we could create the shape of our reality.

The others didn't stand a chance. Our enthusiasm was just too much for them. Our excitement was too self-contained. The other women seemed so glad of it. The other men soon gave up on it. In time we were totally alone—even at the height of the day. Even when the boat had arrived. But that day we had hiked to the waterfall was one of our best. The women just loved it there. It was their idea that we swim naked in that clear pool which swelled with their nipples, exciting our possibilities. Making us all *reach out and touch, hold, swim, at one point even embrace as if we were one. As if the true meaning had at last begun!*

But how do I get into that? How do I explain the . . . dimen-

sions of our relationship—the domains that were established? Not just between Julian and me, or between Pam and Dianne—but even Dianne and I had our *relationship. And Julian and Pam had* theirs. *And Pam and I had another. And Dianne and Julian another. And so every way we turned we* each *of us yearned for that part which belonged to us all.*

That place which contained the electricity.

As if we were part of some . . . generator!

And then came the night Julian mentioned the mescaline.

"We've got two tabs," he said. "We can each take a half."

The two women just looked at each other. It was obvious they weren't overjoyed.

But at the same time they weren't that upset.

"Oh, we've done our share of drugs," Pam said, her eyes turning so big and blue—so suddenly sad. "It's not that. It's just that we're having such a good time. Why take a chance on spoiling it?"

"Yeah," said Dianne. "Why take a chance on—"

"But tomorrow's our last day!" Julian interrupted with a fury. "At least in Yelapa," he said, "and we certainly wouldn't want to take the stuff in Puerto Vallarta. And a half-tab wouldn't do that much—just make us more alive. Just give us another adventure!

"I'm serious," Julian said. "Drugs can be really good sometimes. They can take us places a lot faster. I don't mean hallucinations—I mean awareness of self. I mean if we're really in this together—if we really want *to be together—then this is a good way to do it. . . .*

"All we have to do is move our things to the other end of the beach—away from all the tourists—and spend the day there. We'll take the mescaline in the morning and by dinnertime we'll be hungry as ever to get back to that restaurant in the village. . . .

"Let me put it this way," he said. "How many chances in our lives will we get to go so deep, in such a perfect place, with so many people we like so much?"

He paused. He looked at each of us separately. Never had I seen such fervor in his eyes.

Even the women recognized a kind of . . . religion there.

"Don't you see?" Julian said. "It's just like going up that waterfall—that same feeling. Only this time it'll be inside us!"

How could we refuse him that? How could we refuse ourselves? In a flash we looked at each other and recognized that something else was going on here—that that drug was some kind of . . . communion. That what he was offering was—himself!

God how we loved him for that.

God how we loved who we were.

What did it matter if we were naked or clothed—wearing tits or a dick? We had to reach deeper than that.

We had to remain truer, fly faster—go as far as the light would permit!

Which brings me to the opening of act three—our final full day in Yelapa. Followed by two days in Puerto Vallarta. All of them really one epoch, thanks to that drug which just wouldn't quit . . .

That feeling which swept us away. . . .

Julian advised us against breakfast. He said it would rob us of the drug. He said our bodies should be pure, clean—ready to admit the experience. "Now I know this is good stuff," he said. "But half a tab shouldn't make us crazy."

But half a tab on an empty stomach in a foreign country in the early morning was a little more than we had bargained for. We became downright silly. We laughed at everything. Julian said he had to take a piss and we thought it was the funniest thing we had ever heard—the sound of it. The splash of it in the ocean.

We made up words. We created games. We took close-ups of Dianne's tits. We needed no excuses to touch. Anything was possible. Everything was forgivable. "Responsibility," Pam said to us at one point, and then giggled. "That's what we have—responseability!" And then she took off all her clothes and jumped into the ocean.

God did we laugh.

But then something happened. Allofasudden it happened. In the middle of a Frisbee toss I heard a noise inside. Like the crack of a mirror inside. I remember dropping instantly and clutching my knees and rocking with the ocean and trying to hold it together. Trying to stop it from splitting. But then Julian was beside me and Pam was beside him. And Dianne was kissing me. I think she was . . . licking me. I remember I was suddenly on a spaceship and everything was happening very slowly. As if it took eighteen years to cross a room.

And then it was afternoon. The boat was anchored in the inlet. The other end of the beach was packed with tourists. The four of us were huddled in a circle in our makeshift "tent"—blankets and bamboo—just looking at each other. Studying each other. Our skins so dark from the sun. Our eyes so alive from the contrast. Julian at noon, Pam at three, me at six, Dianne at nine—in touch with a clockwork precision.

A vision still frozen in time.

And then Dianne asked a question: "What does it mean to die?"

Don't ask me where she got it, but it seemed to belong there.

As if she were asking, "What does it mean to truly live?"

It started a round of discussion—of words and feelings and physical reactions that took us . . . someplace I dare not travel. Certainly not tonight.

It's getting so late. The fog is so thick.

But I do remember at one point Julian amended Dianne's question.

"What does it mean to choose to die?" he asked her. "What does it mean to take your own *life?"*

And then he was talking about masturbation. About a game he sometimes played with himself. About how he pretended his dick was a gun and when it went off everything would be over. His entire life would be over.

And he was talking to Dianne. Directly to Dianne.

Right away I thought I recognized a horror in Pamela's eyes. A sudden panic, as if she wanted out of there—away from her drug. For the first time I felt as if I were already back in San Francisco—or as if some part of it had suddenly appeared here. But Dianne somehow understood. Her tits swelled with a deep breath that soothed us all. She reached out like a madonna and took Julian in her arms as she spoke very softly.

"It must be so exciting to believe it," she told him. "To force yourself not to come. To stop at the last *second. To be so full of life—so close to death—at once!"*

That night at the restaurant went by in a blink: with several glasses of wine. That next day on the boat went by like a song: with several rounds of margaritas. Even the band on board seemed to play to us.

Even the throngs of tourists seemed to revolve around us.

There was something about the way we looked, and the way we arrived in Puerto Vallarta—as if we belonged together. As if we were separately *in love together. Dianne and I were so much shorter that we appeared to be a couple. And Julian and Pam were both so tall, so blond and blue-eyed that they could have been brother and sister.*

Or husband and wife.

"Whatever it is," Dianne whispered to me at Carlos O'Brian's that afternoon, "even the waiters seem to give it more authority. Why, look at them—it's as if they've assigned a meaning to us."

And it was true. I could feel it.

I could remember what it was like before we met the women—how we had to be more cautious then.

How two men couldn't have too *much fun together.*

But now it was different—now we were part of something so true that it couldn't be defined. So close to death that it had *to be alive.*

Julian knew it better than any of us. He lavished the knowledge on me. He made it seem as if he were only with me—even with them.

Even through them.

Every word that day was intimate. Even our laughter contained its layers. Every time Julian brushed my arm, or touched me under the table, it was as if some tiny . . . miracle had occurred. Some gentle nudging of . . . liberation. For the first time since the women's big speech I heard the word gay *mentioned—this time by me. I couldn't help myself. I was feeling so good from the boat ride, from the late-afternoon tequila—from that drug which echoed with each sip I took—that I wanted it to be spoken. It didn't matter that things were understood. "My life is words," I told them. "Sometimes it just helps me to . . . form things."*

And so I did—right there at Carlos O'Brian's. Over two more rounds of margaritas. Tales of adventure! Of Secret Identities! Of porno peek-machines!

Tales of Julian and Robert. . . .

And so it came to pass: the women responded in turn. Not right away—but later that day at our hotel. And all the next day on the beach. It came out gradually, like sand sifted through fingers—the fact they felt they were "different." The feeling that somehow they were . . . queer.

"We're objects," Dianne said at one point, applying her suntan lotion with venom. "Fuckees!" she called it. "Products of other people's expectations—and expectorations!"

"Nearly twenty-five years old and we're not even married," Pamela said. "Certainly no children. For Dianne a high-school abortion. For me a broken engagement to a doctor. To a doctor*!*

"You should have heard my mother," she said. "You'd think I had rejected her. *You'd think I had cut her heart out!"*

"Maybe the problem is that we're just too good-looking," Dianne said. "That just too *many men want us. It's so hard to find love when you're always being pounced upon."*

"Listen," Pamela said very seriously. "You tell us what it's like to be gay and I tell you it's just the same to be straight. We're all of us being hounded by images of how the world should fit together.

"I'll tell you the truth," she added, suddenly changing direction, allowing the sun to hit her back. "If you guys weren't gay we'd gobble you up in a minute. You wouldn't stand a chance."

"But that's just the point," Dianne said. "If they weren't gay then they wouldn't be who they are. Things wouldn't be the same. None of this would exist for any of us.

*"God do I love what we have," she admitted to us all. "But it's nothing but a moment—*this *moment. So what are we doing talking about the rest of our lives? Tomorrow you'll go back to San Francisco and we'll go back to St. Louis and it'll be over. Even if we see each other again someday it won't be the same. It can't be the same. That's the one thing I can say for certain I've learned this past week. . . .*

"So to hell with it," she said, suddenly standing up. "We've got so little time left. Tonight's our last night and we've got to do something amazing—something completely different. Whaddya say we . . . go dancing!" she said. "That's it—we'll work *it out of us. We'll* sweat *it out of us. We'll take our last moments together and turn them into . . . a song. Into . . . an art! It'll be something so spectacular that we'll blow ourselves away. We'll blow the* world *away. Whaddya say?"*

And with that she suddenly turned around and skipped happily, almost childishly into the ocean. . . .

And then it was night. As now it is night.

Everyone's gone inside glass—except for a shape in the shadows.

I can see it smoking a cigarette.

I can see the flicker of coals—the burning of ash—but nothing that hides behind it.

Nothing of substance or form.

It's so dark out here I can barely see the pages in front of me.

And yet I must go on—I must go back.

I must get it out of me quickly: the dreams, the words, the motion, that flow. . . . The fact it almost was over.

The fact it's ending again!

The women were dressed to kill.

We could see them across the lobby.

They were all in white, both in silk, with skirts that clung to their contours. With eyes like mother-of-pearl.

With hair hung loose and purses held tight they were creatures of obvious dimension. Objects of everyone's attention.

Especially as they climbed into a cab.

Especially when we got to the disco.

All those Mexican men outside hooting and hollering and hoping to pick up a woman were suddenly speechless.

What do you say to a vision?

You accept it as out of your grasp.

How do you approach a miracle?

You allow it to enter inside.

They both were tremendously pleased. They thought it had something to do with us. They imagined that Julian and I had somehow tamed the crowd, parted the waters, escorted a . . . feeling inside.

Even at Carlos O'Brian's things had never been quite this perfect. Even at that restaurant in Yelapa, that night we had taken the drug, things had never been quite this . . . high.

Even now, as I light another cigarette—as I echo that other burning signal in the night—I know I must return as if to childhood.

As if to . . . church.

To that feeling I always used to get after confession—after making a devout act of contrition . . .

After handing the priest my sins and watching him tear them up, throw them away . . .

The disposal of evil, then walking outside—can you understand it? Can you understand my wanting to get hit by a car so I would be saved—so I would be contained forever in that one moment?

Do I make any sense about how hard we held on that night? About how fast we danced and how much we laughed that night?

Can you understand that you're *part of it too—you who are me from the future . . .*

Like that man over there in the shadows!

I know that something's going on because every time I draw on my cigarette he immediately draws on his. Or is it the other way around?

Is it what Brian would call . . . Relativity?

Is it what Julian would call . . . a complicity?

And . . . why am I so sure it's a man?

And why am I suddenly scared?

And . . . maybe we should get out of here.

Maybe we should go have a drink with Brian.

I know he's working tonight.

I can put you back in my knapsack and carry you over my shoulder and take you inside The Arena.

And then go back to that disco.

From bar to bar—as if in music.

Whaddya say?

Whaddya think?

But no—I can't go there. I can't go writing inside a bar! People would think I'm crazy. People would think I'm . . . driven.

That dance floor was such a setup.

It dominated the center of the room.

It was surrounded on all sides by speakers and lights, lasers and sounds that could have been in New York.

And yet everyone was dressed so Mexican. In colors and prints that created havoc on the dance floor.

That's one reason the women stood out.

Especially when they started to sweat.

Especially when the black lights flashed on.

Suddenly the colors got darker and the whites got brighter and . . . they actually seemed to glow.

As if those dresses were made of neon.

As if those women were more than naked.

You should have seen the way people stared.

And not just at them—but at us. At Julian and me. As if we were really macho.

As if we had dick going down to our ankles!

There was just no way to ignore it.

Especially when we headed back to our table.

Julian would guide Pam and I would put my arm around Dianne as if I owned her. And she loved it.

And we did it.

Again and again we went back to that dance floor, then back to our drinks—usually all of us together. But sometimes just Julian and Pam. And sometimes just me and Dianne. And one time there was a slow song and it didn't matter that Pam was so much taller—I wanted to dance with her. *I wanted to hold her and move her and touch her in front of everyone. And so we switched off.*

And then we switched back.

And then there was a familiar song that caused the two women to shriek and pull each other up and skip off to the dance floor together. And that's when Julian smiled.

And so I smiled back.

And so he said, "Do you wanna dance?"

And I couldn't believe it! For a moment the music stood still.

For a second the beat lasted forever . . .

But then I realized he was joking.

I watched him reaching nervously for a cigarette as he forced a laugh and tried to get out of it.

But suddenly I was serious.

In an instant I recognized it had taken two weeks and two women to achieve this moment. So how could I let it escape?

I had *to reach out quickly and intercept his flame.*

"Who do we know here?" I said. "What does it really matter?"

I looked him dead in the eyes. I could see the man in the shadows.

"C'mon," I said. "Let's do it. Let's be real. Let's make this night really mean something."

I remember tugging hard on his hand. I remember pulling him up and looking in his eyes and putting out his cigarette and . . . I'm still not sure how it happened.

There's just no simple way to explain it.

It's so much later now.
So much can happen between paragraphs now.

"I think I love you," I remember I told him.
"I think you . . . have to," I remember he said.

And then it was him reaching out.
Leading me *to the dance floor.*
To that . . . feeling of hope.
To these . . . sliding glass doors.
And . . .

Even the women were stunned.
You'd think we had physically attacked them.
You'd think they were no longer sexy.
Suddenly everyone stopped dancing.
If only we could have been labeled.
If only it could have been expected.
But the women had made us legitimate.
And the drinks had made us so high.
And the Quaaludes are still on my desk.
And the mescaline is still in my mind.
And . . .

Now he's in the bathroom.
His clothes are in front of the mirror.
The mirror is beside the bed.
I just heard him turn off the shower.
I just heard him call out my name.
And . . .

The word became flesh.

And . . .

The shadow became man.

And . . .

At last we are back where we started.

At last I can put you away!

Nothing is ever what it appears to be when you look at it close up. I'm a little older now and things no longer contain that kind of immediacy. The manuscript which began in a gym and that journal which ended in Mexico are one and the same to me now. It doesn't matter whether Julian was legend or simply headline—that moment on the dance floor and that moment at the café are both long behind me. I return for one reason only: to set time and record straight. And to tell you in truth it was terrible.

Of course everything I write now is an extension of that journal which keeps coming back to me. Just when I think all is lost I read it and see something new. I treat each page as a relic—some curious omen that traveled through time and a cab to reach me. Such things do not happen by accident.

But listen to me! You'd think I were no longer in front of sliding glass doors. You'd think I were in another city, or another country—looking at a landscape which no longer has any connection. But in truth almost nothing has changed. Except for a beard I look almost no different than I did in those paragraphs and photographs of Mexico. And yet I feel somehow . . . removed, as if witnessing the return of a spaceship. As if there are people on board I know and love and yet they don't seem to recognize me. For them it has been only hours, but for me it has been my life.

And tonight . . . well, tonight something very bizarre happened at the pool hall. It's what prompted me to return to this typewriter after so long an absence. It's what made me realize things would not be over until I had concluded them on paper. There are still some blank pages in that notebook, of course, but for some reason it is . . . behind me now. I cannot simply attach these words as if they are a part of it when the very fabric of my life has changed. I have even rearranged the furniture. My desk now faces the window. The light hovers above it and as I look out I can see this page rising out of my typewriter like a tombstone. The darkness has created a reflection. My ghostly image looks back from the glass as if from a negative. The moon is whole in my mind and the fog is thick in my eyes and I know it's all inside me. My image contains the night.

I no longer need any mirrors.

Even the one in the bathroom—I had it taken down.

I just don't want to look at myself anymore.

At least not in living color.

That's why I'm growing a beard.

That's why I quit the gym.

During the day I sleep.

At night I inhabit the darkness.

On Thursdays I go to the pool hall.

The sailor of course doesn't recognize me.

Outside the neon glows red and hot in the cold night. It says PALACE ILLIARDS—the B is still burned out—and it marks the point where Turk and Mason converge on Market Street, pouring people like tears from The Tenderloin.

It's open twenty-four hours a day, seven days a week, fifty-two weeks a year, thirty-seven steps above the vomit-stained pavement.

Inside the only light is fluorescent. There are no windows. It is very much like the porno bookshop. Day and night are identical and the only weather is a cloud of cigarette smoke. It swirls like fog over islands of green felt. It swims past the pinball wizards, the pool sharks, the man selling joints of Colombian grass for a dollar—past Lock-up Jack and The Ghost and The Hungarian and The Iceman ("He's so cold he's got ice water in his veins. He never smiles and he never talks and he never loses. It's winter all around him").

It's a strange place—a place where most people have nicknames. Where nobody has a last name.

The clock on the wall has pool balls for numbers. The carpet is pink and faded, scarred by cigarettes and time. The coffee counter is lined with men sitting next to each other, alone. The mammoth room is mirrored on three sides, splattering images like pool balls—bouncing off of each other, into each other, into the shape of games to be played. And bets to be made.

But I don't look at the mirrors anymore.

I concentrate hard on my game.

I concentrate hard on the sailor.

I carry a tiny tape recorder in my pocket.

I try to find out all I can about where they used to go together. About what they used to do together.

It's morbid, I know—and tonight it was even . . . violent.

The sailor was so visibly shaken that I felt sorry for him.

He had come to trust me. He had come to like me. And then . . .

And now . . .

"She couldn't get enough," he was saying as he hit the five ball into the side pocket. "She had had us all in various combinations and had paid well for it, but she was never really satisfied until Julian came to town."

He took the cigarette out of the corner of his mouth.

"Not that he had just arrived," he was saying, "but for a long time he kept his distance from anyone as blatant as Desire. At least that's what she called herself."

He surveyed the pool table as if it were landscape.

"I don't know how many times she approached him, but one night I overheard her offer him a flat fifty bucks and he turned it down. 'You don't need me,' he told her. 'You need a fuckin' dildo.' "

He put the cigarette back in his mouth.

He leaned over the table.

His shirtsleeves were rolled up.

I could see the tattoo of an anchor on his arm.

"Need—that's the word that grabbed me," he was saying. "In this business it's all want. But Julian was different. He never hung out at hustler bars. And on the streets he wasn't like the rest of us. That much was obvious from some of the losers he went home with. Of course he had to be paid something, that's part of the game, but for him it was also . . ."

He closed one eye.

". . . a *feeling,*" he said as he sank the three ball. "A feeling that the person was *desperate.* Not desperate like Desire for the act, but for . . . the flesh. For the presence of another . . . *person* inside."

He paused and reached for some chalk.

He rubbed it on his hands and the cue stick.

One by one he was cleaning up the table.

There were only three of his balls left, and then the eight ball, and I couldn't help hoping he would win.

The better he played the faster he talked.

"Anyway, the night he finally gave in to Desire was the night of our first real encounter. It was a Thursday, I remember, and he had seen me often enough to know who I was but neither of us had ever spoken. But when he saw Desire heading his way he suddenly crossed the street and offered me a cigarette and even before it was lit she was on him. Begging for him. Urging him to go home with her. Offering him a hundred bucks and as much cocaine as he could snort.

"Everybody knew she dealt the stuff. A lot of the guys on the street were her best customers. Very often it was a trade—tit for tat, so to speak. You fill her cunt, she fills your nose. That's obviously where she got her money and she wasn't a bad looker. She smelled a little funny and she wore too much makeup and she had these two big warts at the corner of her mouth but as street life goes she was one of the best lays around. Julian was probably the first one who had ever turned her down and at the beginning she was really pissed. And then she got more and more . . . desperate. I mean the kind of desperate Julian seemed to thrive upon. I mean suddenly she was crying and screaming and clawing at him with her long fingernails. Scratching his cheek and drawing blood. And her eyes were so wild and her warts seemed so big and . . . that's when it happened. I couldn't believe it! The way he held both her hands in one of his and slapped her really hard across the face. What a noise it made. I can still hear it echoing down the streets. And then he slammed her against a building and pushed his body against hers and said 'OK, cunt, I just hope you can handle this.'

"What a moment that was! The look she gave him, as if she couldn't *wait.* As if she were willing to do it right there on the dirty streets. And when Julian grabbed me by the arm and pulled me along but didn't say a word I knew it would be spectacular. I didn't even ask how much my cut would be. Julian had acquired such a reputation for his mystery on the streets—for his *separateness* from the rest of us—that this unspoken invitation was too deliberate to refuse. I knew he had singled me out as a partner, a sort of Robin to his Batman, heading toward a diabolical confrontation that would have consequence for the entire world. I don't think I had ever been more excited.

"But listen to me!" he was saying, slamming one ball into another ball that caused a chain reaction which sank two of his balls and completely redistributed mine.

All he had left was the eight ball but he ignored it.

He was looking directly at me.

"I shouldn't be telling you any of this," he was saying. "I don't know what it is about you. You seem to demand so much and yet you say so little. And yet I like you for some reason. In a way you remind me of . . . *him.*"

He had no direct line of fire to the eight ball. He would have to bank the cue ball off the far end of the table, making it bounce back and strike the eight ball at a precise angle that would drive it into a corner pocket. It was an almost impossible shot.

I quickly pulled a bill out of my pocket.

I slammed it on the table.

I didn't want to seem too anxious to hear about Julian.

"Five says you can't make it," I said.

"You're on," he answered, and was immediately very quiet. Reaching again for the chalk. Concentrating entirely on his shot. Giving me a moment to feel somehow . . . guilty. As if that tape recorder were a weapon.

As if I should have warned him I was armed.

But I know what happens when people find out they're being recorded. I've interviewed enough people to know they don't talk the same. They don't even think the same. They give you what they imagine you want, not what they are. I had no choice but to play my own game with the sailor. And to execute it as deliberately as he was about to execute that shot.

Of course I knew he would make it.

When challenged he always rose to the occasion.

It was a way of paying for my sins.

I didn't have to feign my disgust.

"I give up!" I can hear myself saying, then slamming my pool stick on the table. "Let's get the hell out of here and go smoke a joint."

How thorough is my lie as I listen to it.

Yes, listen to it. I am there and here at once. I wear earphones that surround me with tonight. I turn up the volume and I can hear things I completely missed before. It is like going back and searching for clues. That tape recorder was so tiny it fit into my shirt pocket and yet it picked up everything. Even the background noise. Horns beeping and footsteps echoing down the streets. Even the sounds of our breaths as we inhaled deeply and held them as long as we could. Passing the joint back and forth. Turning corners and circling the block and returning eventually to the pool table, but getting higher with each step we took.

"Don't you see?" the sailor was saying. "That night everything changed. Not just for Desire—but for me. Julian had picked us *both* up. *He* was in control. Even the cocaine responded to his touch. I'll never forget the way he licked his fingers and dipped them into the cocaine and then applied it to her cunt. And then to his dick. And then to *my* dick. And then to her tongue and lips and warts and throat.

"Damn did she get excited!" he was saying. "There were mirrors all around her bed. She refused to dim the lights. She wanted to see it all. She wanted to have us both. She loved the idea of his applying the drug directly to our sex, actually coating it. Electrifying it. Getting *it* rather than us high. As if he were teaching us what it meant to—'have' sex!" he was saying.

"To . . . *be* sex!" he was saying.

"She took my dick in her mouth as she squeezed her legs

together. But Julian forced them apart. He shoved himself inside. He stuffed it as if into a socket. His every thrust jolted her harder against my dick—sending it deeper into her throat—until finally it seemed as if Julian and I were . . . *meeting* inside. Actually touching inside her body!

"It was like something out of a porno movie," he was saying. "For a moment I imagined cameras hidden behind her mirrors. Everywhere I looked I saw eyes looking back as if through peek machines. I knew we weren't alone. I knew that Julian had somehow brought . . . the *future* into that moment.

"Even *you* into that moment!

"And yet what I'm talking about happened between *us,*" he was saying. "Between *me* and Julian.

"*Through* Desire.

"She was the one holding us, containing us, even paying us—but what really occurred had nothing to do with her.

"I realized it the moment we stepped outside.

"I realized it when Julian took that hundred-dollar bill and ripped it in two—giving half of it to me.

"He didn't say a word because he didn't have to.

"It was understood that we both would have what neither of us could spend!

"Do you understand what I mean?" the sailor was saying, and then pausing. Actually waiting for a response.

But what could I say?

All these weeks of trying to pull something out of him and suddenly it was pouring out of him.

I didn't like it.

I didn't trust it.

I reached for the joint as we turned a corner and walked the final block in silence.

I can still hear a siren sweeping past us in the night.

I can still hear the neon digesting as we walked beneath the huge sign that said PALACE ILLIARDS.

He's a hustler, I kept telling myself. A *sometimes* sailor. A man of the streets and night.

His every instinct implies *deceit,* I kept telling myself.

And yet what happened as I racked up the balls took me completely by surprise.

I couldn't believe his sudden sentimentality.

His tears just didn't belong there.

Even The Iceman noticed them.

Even The Hungarian halted his game.

"I loved him," the sailor was saying as he reached inside his wallet. "Every Thursday night I loved him through somebody else."

He pulled out that torn fragment of a hundred-dollar bill as he would a piece of shrapnel. As he would an old photograph.

He slammed it furiously on the table.

He looked at me as if he knew who I was.

"C'mon," he said, looking me right in the eyes. "Let's make this game really mean something."

And then he . . .

And now I . . .

But . . . listen. You can hear it happening in that machine. As if it *is* in that machine. As if it's not just in my mind but—at my fingertips. I know I have the power to turn it off. To walk away from it. To go to bed or pet the cat or . . . change the tape. Give you Julian himself! But . . .

Listen. Listen with your eyes. There's more going on than meets the ears. So much happened after Mexico, before the shrapnel—between the mirrors. I had no choice but to . . . confront him tonight.

End it tonight.

Show him the bill in *my* pocket tonight.

The one that matched his tonight!

Can you hear the look on his face?
Can you see the scream in his eyes?

Can you understand the confusion? His fear? The violence? That . . . tape recorder!

It flew out of my pocket when he struck me.

It hit the wall and landed on the faded carpet beside me.

He had knocked me down, he was about to kick me, when suddenly he realized what it was.

What it meant.

I could see cop written all over his face. I could see narc or detective or reporter or . . . *entrapment* written all over his face.

Suddenly my questions made sense.

Immediately his danger was *real.*

In seconds the entire room was in turmoil. Even The Ghost disappeared quickly toward the stairs. And the man selling joints swiftly followed.

On the tape it sounds like a stampede.

As if someone had shouted out an order. Or given out an odor. Or a signal. Or a warning. Or . . .

A *reason*—that's what the sailor was looking for! That's why he stood motionless, as if in terror, looking at me and my machine.

At what I had done.

At how it had seemed *before* I pulled that bill out of my pocket.

Before those two halves created a hole so deep it nearly destroyed us.

It certainly *defined* us.

It made us see the crime was not deception—but desecration.

And not against him—but against Julian!

What happened next I'm not even sure. As I struggled to my feet I felt dizzy. I realized blood was oozing out of my nose. The side of my head was hurting, actually swelling from where he had struck me, and the sailor was gone. So were both halves of that hundred-dollar bill. So were The Hungarian and Lock-up Jack and just about everybody else except The Iceman and a few others who stood frozen, staring. Wondering what really had happened.

How I got out of there I'm still not sure. The last thing I remember was the clock that had pool balls for numbers. The next thing I knew I was walking the streets. I had somehow gathered up my tape recorder, probably displaying it like a badge as I inserted it into my pocket and stepped with authority toward the door—but somewhere along the line I had lost. I had lost what counted most at a place like PALACE ILLIARDS—my anonymity. My Secret Identity.

The *game.*

• • •

Believe me when I say we are alone now. It's 1:00 A.M. and no phones will ring. No sliding glass doors will open like wounds or lead like fences toward Brian. Even the tape recorder offers little solace anymore. What happened when we got back from Mexico was—and still is—inside *me.* Not a machine. Not a typewriter or a generator or even that camera that trapped the light—transported the motion to San Francisco. . . .

In a way it was a new beginning, like the time I first arrived here. Back when my notebook was blank. Before I had any mirrors. In a way it was like arranging it through the mail, having everything ready ahead of time—only this time it included a lover. At last I can use that word.

At last I can say it's true.

Even Digit seemed somehow to notice it, go along with it—actually get into it. Before Mexico he had always kept a certain distance from Julian, refusing to get too close, always sleeping on my side of the bed, immediately heading toward the garden or the closet whenever we started having sex. At first I thought it was jealousy mixed with the uncertainty of being an orphan—and of being a cat. And to some extent I was right. Digit could sense the doubt in me. The electricity jolted both of us whenever Julian's telephone rang.

But it was more than that which changed after Mexico. It was Julian himself that Digit instinctively responded to. It was the way Julian burst through those sliding glass doors and swept Digit into his arms, laughing gently as he pulled out a tiny straw sombrero he had bought in Puerto Vallarta. Immediately Digit started purring, sniffing—allowing Julian to attach that tiny sombrero under the chin. Other cats would have struggled to get out of it. But after two weeks of living out of doors, of depending on Brian for food, of returning to our apartment and always finding it empty, Digit seemed transformed—as if he had undergone a change as profound as ours. No longer was he some fugitive presence lurking somewhere in the backdrop of our lives, but instead he was a real . . . force. Almost . . . a child. Suddenly prancing across the baby tears and climbing atop the wooden fence with a sense of obvious satisfaction. Allowing us to take several photographs that we later attached to the refrigerator. That are still attached to the refrigerator.

In many ways those first few weeks were the purest of them all. The most gentle, the most loving of our relationship. That's why Digit responded so instinctively. Not only was there a vitality to the way we looked, to our deep tans and our sun-bleached hair—but it inhabited our very motion. What we chose to do. The way we moved and talked. As if we still were tourists. Even acting still like tourists. Riding cable cars, walking through Chinatown, going to Fisherman's Wharf, eating shrimp out of paper cups—turning corners and discovering worlds and finding it so easy to touch, laugh, talk, point, enjoy anything that was new.

And everything was new.

Even places we knew well—places like the gym—were as magical as that waterfall in Yelapa. Nowhere was it more apparent that Julian had undergone a transformation. His very muscles seemed to speak the news. He had been away from those weights for only two weeks and yet I could see his body had somehow . . . softened. Become more natural. Not that he was no longer taut or sculpted—he couldn't have changed that much in such a short time—but somehow the hardest lines were gone. And the separations between his muscles weren't quite so severe. And so he seemed more whole, more complete—even more honest than before.

Certainly more beautiful than before.

Yes, Mexico was still inside both of us—right here in our own city. Beneath fluorescent lights. And yet I dared not question it. I dared not ask why it was happening—how it could be he was ignoring the eyes which surrounded us in that gym; which contained us together in a shape more stunning than anything I could have imagined. Right away I realized it went deeper than the mirrors—beyond even that painted blue shell on the wall—to a place where every image contained a new set of reflections . . .

Where every answer contained a new set of questions which had something to do with that dance floor: with the gravity of Mexico, as if I were a moon and Julian were some planet and we couldn't help but obey the laws of that universe. . . .

It was easier to look at it that way—in a scientific way—rather than assigning it mythic proportions. Or even sexual proportions. For what was Julian if he wasn't a man? And what was Robert if he wasn't a man? Is the answer to that question *woman?*

Is that what those eyes on the dance floor were looking for?

Is that what those eyes in the mirrors were staring at?

And what about Julian's telephone—why was it that it so seldom rang anymore?

Why was it that he wouldn't go out without me anymore?

Where was the old man now? Where was the sailor now?

Where was *Desire* now?

My God, I think I'm lost. I'm trying to explain how it ended and suddenly I'm . . . starting again. The harder I travel a straight line the more it seems to spiral. If only I could attribute it to one thing—to one place or point in time—then you would understand it all. You would realize that I was not with the sailor tonight, but with Julian tonight—following him as I had always followed him tonight. That's all I was doing—just keeping him alive. Just keeping him *inside.* Even the bad moments. Even the desperate moments. Whatever he had been with or without me, with or without that sailor—before or after Mexico—I wanted it tonight. I need it now with you. I need to convince myself that it's something worth going back to, worth even dying through, with whoever I decide you are tonight. . . .

Don't you see? He was pulling me so subtly into his world that I didn't even recognize it. What was once his power to attract was becoming our power to attract—like Julian and the sailor. Even the streets and bars; even Brian was accessible to us now—accessible to us as a team now. We went to The Arena together, standing in that same spot at the end of the bar that I had once occupied so selfishly—and so solitary in my abandon. Poor Brian didn't know what to make of it. No longer was there a way for me to explain it to him. No longer could I wait until he locked up the bar and swept me into the world of his mind. It was funny, in a way—the sense of loss I suddenly felt, as if there had been a reversal. As if all I ever really wanted was what I couldn't have.

But of course that wasn't true. I wanted to be there with Julian. I loved the attention he lavished on me. He was what every man in The Arena openly desired—and he was mine. There was no pretense about it. There were no games going on. It was obvious we weren't there to pick anybody up, but simply to have a good time. At least it was obvious to me—which goes to show you how little I really knew about Julian.

Which goes to show you how very much in love I was.

It's just that I was so certain of Julian now. No matter where we went I wasn't afraid of losing him anymore. Digit *was* our child. That apartment and that garden and even those mirrors were our home. We lived not only in it—but for it. For a brief period everything happened as if in a storybook. Even our sex was too good to be true. All Julian had to do was look at me and my whole body came alive in response. And he knew it. And he wanted it. And I was just so happy that it was happening—that at last we were having what I had always hoped it would be possible for two men to have—a kind of holiness.

Or rather, *whole*-liness.

As if something had been spoken.

Or prayed!

But it hadn't—not with words. But one cannot be truly loved—*be* the beloved—without feeling it. Trusting it. Ignoring all the danger signals. Ignoring even the warnings of Brian as I sat at that bar, watching Julian at the pool table; watching him win game after game, night after night—holding the spotlight as he was challenged by all the "boys" in that room. That's what they seemed like—boys, not men. Not anything strong enough to take Julian away from me. "Listen," I finally told Brian as he served me a drink one night. "You weren't with us. You don't know what happened in Mexico. I'm not even sure I know what happened in Mexico. But I do know if I don't believe in it—blindly, totally, as I would in a God—then it doesn't have a hope in hell of ever working out."

It wasn't until the words were out of me that I realized with what strength I had spoken them. I realized in that moment that I had made a commitment. I realized that that commitment—not Julian himself—was what I was holding on to. I realized so much in that moment about giving and taking; about making choices; about keeping them choices by renewing them every minute—re*choice*ing every second—but Brian had no idea what I was talking about. . . .

He looked at me as if I had accused him of something.

He took my money and headed toward the cash register much too slowly, much too deliberately.

When he returned with my change and placed it on the bar his eyes seemed so dark—so fiercely distant.

And then he did something I had never seen him do before. He immediately picked up the tip I had left and forced it into his pocket. Actually stuffed it there as his eyes settled sadly, as if knowingly, on the shape of a tall, blond man—a man who looked very much like Julian—who was racking up balls at the far end of the pool table. . . .

I should have realized right then that something was wrong. I should have known that nothing escapes Brian at The Arena. I should have trusted that distant look in his eyes rather than remaining so high on my own certainty. Never once did I suspect that Julian's refusal to talk about us—to put our relationship into words—was anything but a choice. How could I have called it an inability?

How dare I imply it was . . . a weakness.

I'm half tempted to leap ahead—only one night ahead—to when Julian would stand in that same bar, at that same pool table, with that same blond man who looked so much like him—who acted so much like him—and start screaming for me to get out of there. To leave him alone! To . . .

But wait. I'll come back to that. I'll move ahead to that. There's no need to go too fast right now. I've got the whole night ahead of me. I've got my whole future ahead of me. I've got Digit right here beside me—to remind me. Please bear with me. Please stand by. Please realize I never for an instant thought it was anything more than what the man said it was—a ride home.

A joint on the way.

All three of us in the front seat.

Julian in the middle.

The mention of a hot tub. . . .

"I've got some really great cocaine," the man was saying. "I've been snorting it all night and it's really got me wired. Why don't you guys come by and keep me company for a while?"

The thing was I liked him. That's probably why it eventually hurt so much. He said his name was Phaedrus and right away I exploded into laughter. Julian didn't get it. The man seemed so surprised I recognized it. "Phaedrus was a student of Socrates," I explained. "A character from the Platonic dialogues. He was searching for the meaning of love."

I looked at the man and smiled.

I remembered the night in Florida when I was Holden Caulfield.

"C'mon," I said. "What's your real name?"

But it was true. He insisted his parents had had a fight. They couldn't agree on a name and so they pulled a book at random off a shelf and there it was—the Modern Library edition of *The Works of Plato,* complete with a table of contents which listed, among others, *Phaedrus, Lysis, Crito,* and *Protagoras*—eventually with the last name of Reilly.

His voice was hearty and genuine, yet somehow innocent. It reminded me in a way of Pamela—Pamela on the seashore. . . . He pulled into the driveway of a large Victorian house, switched off the ignition, sat for a moment in silence, and then—as if to make a point, as if to prove his authenticity—suddenly said:

"The only problem was my sister. Since all of Socrates' students were male, they ended up calling her Judy."

Right away I capsized into giggles—echoing the man's own furious laughter—and Julian didn't know what to make of us. (He had no idea that Phaedrus reminded me so much of a cab driver who had once delivered me into a palindrome.) Anything that had to do with art—with *literature*—was as remote to Julian as the sailor had been to me, and immediately he got very defensive: calling us "weird"—saying our laughter was phony—and then reaching across my arms, pushing open the door, forcing out his own laugh, and saying something about us hitting the hot tub. . . .

Somewhere inside I must have realized what was happening. Phaedrus wasted no time escorting us into a monstrous library with a huge fireplace and a bear rug that threatened to spring to life before it. He lit the fire, he made us drinks, he brought out the cocaine (and a razor blade) on a mirror the size of a plate, and then he excused himself to go to the back of the house and turn on the hot tub. "It'll take at least a half-hour for it to warm up," he said, "so we may as well make ourselves comfortable."

While Phaedrus was gone Julian sat cross-legged by the fire, placed the mirror on his lap, took the razor blade between his fingers, and chopped the crystals as fine as he could—drawing them into long, thin lines about an inch apart on the glass. In the meantime I surveyed the room: the high ceiling and arched windows; the long rows of shelves with ladders that led to the tops; even, in the far corner, an old rolltop desk that was locked (I tried it) but which had a copy of Thomas Mann's *Death in Venice* planted squarely, as if purposely, on top.

And then it hit me—the room was in such order. I couldn't even find scraps of discarded paper in the wastebasket. There was no notepad near the telephone, no photographs on the wall.

Not even portraits or landscapes—only abstract paintings in earthy tones that matched perfectly the design of the room, as if Phaedrus had intentionally kept himself out of it. Even the books seemed to belong to a collection, not a man. They were very old, all the classics: Chaucer, Shakespeare, the complete Waverley novels, nothing more recent than Melville—not even Twain or Hemingway. Certainly not Updike or Mailer. (Nothing to indicate a preference—a personality.) That's why my eyes kept returning to that copy of *Death in Venice,* which—by virtue of the fact it had been removed from a shelf and, presumably, opened—was the only clue I had to go on.

Yes, *clue* seemed to be the appropriate word, as if there were some mystery going on—some crime about to be committed. For some reason I couldn't help thinking that Phaedrus was not a man, but someone's creation; that Julian was . . . a life; and that whatever was happening here, even Phaedrus' resemblance to Julian, was not accidental.

I don't know how else to explain it.

There is no simple way for me to hand it to you on a platter like the cocaine.

All I know is that I picked up that copy of *Death in Venice* the way Phaedrus' parents must have picked up Plato—with the thought that it contained a portent: something that would speak to me in the present. Whatever page I opened it to—whatever passage my eyes fell upon—it would tell me something about Phaedrus. Somehow I knew it—believed it—opened it—and then heard my name being spoken from the doorway.

I slammed the book shut. I reeled around, like a thief who had been caught in the act, just as Phaedrus dimmed the lights and took several steps toward me. "I see you've discovered my favorite book," he said in a voice that seemed much too serious. "Here," he said, removing the book from my hand, looking me right in the eyes—looking as if into my mind—standing so close that I could see for the first time how much older he was than

Julian: *"Here, let me read you something that always takes my breath away."*

There was something about the way he held the book, opened the book, turned the pages as if he were touching flesh. There was something about the look in his eyes as they arrived on page twenty-four—falling upon the words as if they were landscape. There was something about this man which suddenly reminded me of myself—of that boat ride to Yelapa—of the way my eyes had searched the shoreline as if for salvation. . . .

"Solitude gives birth to the original in us, to beauty unfamiliar and perilous—to poetry," he read in a voice which seemed to come from another time or place—from another corner of that room. *"But also, it gives birth to the opposite: to the perverse, the illicit, the absurd!"*

Why was it he seemed to be speaking so directly to *me*?

Why was it the word *absurd* seemed to turn in on itself—create its own exclamation point?

Suddenly, irreverently, he erupted into laughter that confounded me with the feeling that nothing, not even the thoughts in my head, belonged to me anymore. But before I could understand, let alone respond to what was happening, he was leading me across the room—toward the fireplace and Julian—reaching with one hand into his pocket and keeping it there as if he were clutching a weapon.

Suddenly we were not just crossing a room—but crossing borders. The man who had seemed so young and blond and alive at the pool table was, in a matter of moments, ancient. Every step made him seem older, darker—more demonic. Of course I was high from the joint we had smoked in his car, but even that couldn't explain the feeling of doom that descended like fog down a hillside. Even the fire itself seemed to be part of it—tossing shadows around the room, across the shelves: turning even books into shapes that lived and breathed in the night. By the time we reached Julian I wanted to beg him to leave—to call a cab and get us away from Phaedrus—but I could tell he had already tasted the cocaine: rubbed some of it into his gums, directly onto the membrane: producing an effect as unmistakable as the smile on his face.

Whatever was going to happen here, I decided in that moment, I was not going to run away from it. Instead I sat cross-legged next to Julian on the bear rug and watched Phaedrus pull out a fifty-dollar bill—in a way, a weapon—which he rolled into a tube, inserted into his nose, applied to the cocaine, and then passed on to Julian—who passed it on to me.

My eyes were dilated and my hands were trembling. I could see my image looking back in the glass.

I could feel the fire breathing down my neck.

I knew that Phaedrus hadn't read just a quote—but my mind.

"So now tell me," I said as calmly as I could manage it, looking at Phaedrus as I handed him the cocaine. "What do you do for a living?"

It was a simple enough question—a way of bringing things back to "normal." But little did I know that Phaedrus had undergone a change as profound as mine.

He looked at me as he would an opponent.

"I'm a collector," he said.

"What do you collect?"

"I collect people," he said.

"I'm serious," I said. "This is a great place—you must have money."

"I collect money," he said.

"Are you a writer?" I said.

"I collect death," he said.

"Are you a solitary?"

"Yes. I'm also a solipsist.

"I am alone," he said. "Unlike you and your friend, who is beautiful."

Honest to God. That's exactly the way the conversation went. Even Julian seemed somewhat taken aback by it. And when Phaedrus suddenly exploded into laughter which was high and screechy like a woman's, Julian just looked at me—as if to say the cocaine, no matter how good it was, couldn't be coming on *that* fast. . . .

But it was. I could feel it. I had never had anything quite like it. It made me anxious. It made me aggressive. It seemed to do precisely what Phaedrus intended it to do—make me want more.

Make me feel less.

And so I watched him very carefully, studying his face and exploring his eyes as if I were an artist—searching for detail that could be turned into the shape of what was happening. . . .

But then he winked at me, or rather closed one eye very deliberately—as if he were looking at me under a microscope.

"So now tell me," he then said very slowly, "what do *you* do for a living?"

Immediately I saw my chance to get back.

I took a deep breath.

I smiled at myself in the mirror that was handed me.

"I draw lines," I said. "So does Julian," I said.

And then laughed.

And then sniffed.

And then said:

"We're doodlers. We're degenerates.

"We're not what we appear to be," I said.

"Ah, but you are!" Phaedrus immediately chimed in, turning my words around . . .

Turning my thoughts around.

"You're lovers," he said. "Lovers are always what they appear to be!"

He looked at me precisely the way he had looked at that copy of *Death in Venice.*

He didn't have to tell me he was quoting.

"*Thought that can merge wholly into feeling,*" he said, "*feeling that can merge wholly into thought—these are the artist's highest joy!*"

And then once again he exploded into laughter that was furious—laughter that seemed to know too much as I handed him the fifty-dollar bill which accompanied the mirror.

Which reflected a glance at Julian.

Which made me see why he had brought us here. What we were doing here.

It came crashing in on me like his laughter.

It was as obvious as that bill in his hand!

How had I missed it before?

Suddenly I could see a car on a rampage, a pedestrian at an intersection—a tragedy beyond my control.

"My God, you two know each other!" I heard myself screaming, hardly realizing what I was saying until the words were out of me—until I had glanced at Julian, then glanced at that fifty-dollar bill, then conjured up the image of an old man, of a sailor, of desire. . . .

"You two had this *planned,*" I said, with such venom and conviction that Julian seemed stunned, on the verge of alarm—as if sirens were going off all around us.

But Phaedrus just looked at me with disgust.

He forced out a laugh that was no longer a laugh.

"Don't be ridiculous," he said. "I've never seen either of you before in my life. If I had, you certainly wouldn't be here tonight."

His voice seemed to rise up on hind legs—to claw at the night.

"Who do you think you *are*?" he said. "What makes you think you're so goddamned *important*?" he said.

"Look at you two," he laughed, forgetting the cocaine—turning on Julian as well as myself. "You're infants! You're hardly out of the cradle. You don't know what it means to be perverse, illicit—degenerate.

"You're too young," he said. "You're too beautiful," he said.

"You're not old enough to do anything ugly," he said.

"So don't hand me your crap," he said directly to me. "And don't make it seem as if I lured you here. You came because you wanted my drugs—or my words—or some reflection of yourselves.

"*Well I'm not going to give it to you,*" he said. "I'm not even going to touch you," he said. "I can find that anywhere in this city," he laughed, and suddenly a fierce odor seemed to fill the room.

As if it were coming from his breath.

Or issuing from the drug that was inside me.

"Take a good look at yourselves," he said, howling with laughter. "You're so transparent. You're like windows. You don't have the darkness—the *substance*—to throw anything back. To become mirrors!"

I couldn't believe how quickly his laughter turned to tears.

They just didn't belong there.

I couldn't help pulling away from them.

I couldn't help noticing that Julian seemed attracted to them.

"I just want to absorb you," Phaedrus said very gently, almost pitifully. "I just want to sit here and watch you smile and laugh and tell me about your lives so I can know what you mean to each other," he said. "I just want you to take off your clothes and climb into my hot tub and smoke some more dope and snort some more coke and reach out to each other," he said. "And hold on to each other," he said. "In front of me," he said.

In front of me, he said.

"Answers," he said. "I want answers to questions," he said.

"I want to know where you have traveled—what you have been," he said.

"I want to know which of you is woman," he said.

"I want to see the way you touch and grope and respond to the shape of *you plural,*" he laughed.

"Degenerate," he said. "Perverse and illicit," he cried out. "I will teach you what these *mean,*" he said.

"In time you will know their truth," he said.

"I just want to watch you," he said.

"Take you in my mind. Open you like a book.

"My God, listen to me!" he said—and I *was* listening to him. Watching him as if he were an animal. That wild look in his eyes—that desperate look in his eyes. The kind of look Julian loved. The kind of look the sailor one day would say Julian thrived upon.

How much was going on that I couldn't see.

How much was at stake that I didn't even know about.

Suddenly it seemed more important than ever for me to spring forward—to lash back—to bare fangs and fight for what I knew was mine. Only mine!

But my legs were numb. My arms were dead. Even my hands and lips wouldn't respond as my mind directed them to. It was as if that drug—or maybe Phaedrus' fury—were some anesthetic that had deadened me; that had numbed everything but my consciousness—making me keenly aware and yet utterly defenseless against the scalpel of Phaedrus' tongue as it cut to the very quick of my relationship with Julian.

It was at that moment—at that precise moment—that I looked up in horror and recognized the faraway look in Phaedrus' eyes: the way he suddenly started slurring his words, turning blue, twitching his lips, dripping saliva down his chin—onto the mirror—into that drug which Julian, of all people, must have recognized was not just cocaine, but . . . *angel dust.*

Immediately Phaedrus' voice—not just his words—seemed to belong to some deeper panic: to an ultimate terror that would foretell the death of all of us. (Immediately I remembered articles I had read about angel dust—how it isolates the mind, cuts off brain signals to the organs: how, if enough of it were snorted, the body would simply shut down like a factory—close down the valves, turn off the heart, collapse numbly into a death the mind would comprehend in its entirety: in its enormity—and yet be able to do nothing about.)

"Sex," he said very softly, as if he were going into a trance—looking directly at the fire rather than us (his message as ephemeral as that dance of flame in his eyes). "Isn't that what it's really all about—how we connect with our bodies? Who is the giver, who . . . the receiver.

"Husbands and wives," he said, "mothers and fathers," he said, "have it so easy. Their roles are defined—their children are proof. Their marriage is blessed. Their car insurance is cheaper. Their taxes are cheaper. At the supermarket everything comes in the giant size—the *family* size. Even their parents approve of the reflection—of the aging certainty that life has a meaning. That death plays a part.

"But solitaries," he said, "and all gay people are solitaries," he said—"and all artists are solitaries," he said—"are as alone in their lives as they are in their deaths. They don't have the comfort of approval—the blessings of a church, the license of a society—and so must pay more dearly in every aspect of their lives. In every corner of their search for transcendence!

"Who teaches you how to be gay?" he said. "Who in that world of togetherness even allows for the solitary in life? Who in that family which bred you ever said you could dare dress up in a skirt! Why is it the very notion of woman implies something inferior? Something to be descended upon. A craving—a shame. . . .

"Togetherness!" he howled, erupting into laughter, tears, spit—snot running out of his nose. "Even before I was ten," he said, "even before I knew I was gay," he said, "I sensed that family was not the answer—that Lysis and Crito and Protagoras and Judy were not the answer. That something was missing from the shape of that container—and not even my mother and father could fill the massive, amazingly separate sense that something awful—something *awe-full*—was about to happen with my life.

"Certainly you must understand it," he said. "Certainly you must know it yourselves," he said. "Certainly you must have surmounted the shit that was piled upon you from day one," he said, "when the very first thing they did was pull you from a cunt and look at your dick and assign a direction to your life. A path *they* decided would lead sexually, even violently, but not mentally into that shape from whence you sprang.

"Do you see what I mean?" he said. "Do you see how ingrained it is?" he said. "Can you hear it echoing all around us—in all these books which contain us? In all these words which explain us.

"*Thought*," he said. "Mind," he said. "Flesh," he said. "Roles," he whispered.

"Nothing is real," he said.

"There is so much to break out of in our own heads," he said.

"When you choose to accept man," he said, "when you choose not to accept woman," he said, "you have no choice but to accept the woman *in* you. In *both* of you. In different *parts* of you. In different *times* of you. If you are to survive.

"*If you are to love.*

"That's what I'm searching for!" he said. "That's what I want from you," he said, "the meaning of love. The transcendence of love. The boundaries, the borders, the very biology you must abandon if you are to metamorphose into something deeper, something truer—some strange new creature of the night.

"So go ahead!" he shrieked like a demon. Or a prophet. Or a sorcerer. Or a madman!

"*Be* degenerate," he said. "*Get* hard. Show me what man is! Teach me what love is! That hot tub must be ready by now. The drugs must be upon you by now. Have another drink. Smoke another joint. Pretend I don't exist.

"Pretend you are at home.

"Imagine I am a mirror.

"Imagine you're on a beach.

"Pick your time and place.

"I promise I won't interrupt.

"I promise I won't say a word.

"I just want to watch.

"I just want to inhabit."

And then he fell into silence—a stillness as numb as the night—and I thought I could see what he was talking about.

I thought I knew what he was offering.

I could see a clear pool, a crashing waterfall, orchids blossoming wild in the jungle.

Julian napping naked in the afternoon.

Even waves crashing helplessly onto a beach as it began to make sense.

Too much sense.

Nothing but sense that whatever I chose in my mind—*whatever thought merged wholly into feeling*—Phaedrus would see only sex.

Flesh.

Pornography.

Images flashing frantically inside a peek machine!

But it was more than that. So much more than words and fears which had been hurled like missiles at us. So much more than whether Phaedrus was truly some philosopher or simply a pornographer. Something else happened in that moment—in that swirl—in my mind—in that drug which made me see how very complex everything was. On the one hand I knew Phaedrus' fury was a masquerade—a tactic—part of an elaborate display of laughter and tears that was as deceptive and dangerous as his drugs. (Even the way he seemed to wither away, to draw silently inside himself and all but disappear from that room—allowing Julian and me to confront each other; actually wanting Julian and me to confront each other—seemed to me suspicious: a calculated risk. The maneuver of a voyeur, not a philosopher.)

But on the other hand there was Julian himself. His life-style. All he had ever been with the old man, with the sailor . . . with Mary and Joseph and now this Phaedrus who made me realize, actually decide that what by all logic should be a minor character, *a one-night stand*, had evolved into a major presence: an inescapable fact. An unavoidable symbol of what was again arriving full-circle, full-spiral: delivering us deliberately back to those peeks and clinks behind curtains which closed like eyelids. . . .

But then again I wasn't sure if anything was deliberate. Maybe it was just time for Julian to come into focus. Maybe Phaedrus hadn't so much disappeared from that room as simply withered away in my mind. How could I know what had happened to Phaedrus when it didn't matter what had happened to Phaedrus? When I had no choice but to look at Julian—respond to him. Find out what he was thinking. Approach him with words I dared not speak before. As if Phaedrus had forced us into a position which was, in its own way, already sexual.

"Julian," I said—I remember I said in three swift yet separate syllables—as if I wanted to contain him and yet free him in the same . . .

"Julian," I said—I remember I said but couldn't tell if I was shouting or whispering . . .

"Julian," I remember I think I said to the fire or the man or that wisp of Phaedrus which hung heavy like curtains on . . .

A confessional.

The end of an act.

The fact that I cannot sit here in the future and try to change things.

For isn't it the same thing—my writing this down?

Your being here now.

Aren't you Phaedrus?

Isn't that what this is really all about?

Julian, stop. Listen to that drug. It must be doing to you what it's doing to me. Suddenly I feel as if I'm wearing ear-plugs—as if the world is shut out, or as if the universe is shut inside me, and the only thing I can hear is the beat of my heart. The expanse of my breath. The rush of my blood. The rivers and canyons and currents of . . . my mortality.

Julian, look at me now. See *who I am without you. I'm a child, Julian. I'm afraid for my life, Julian. It's as if I'm in a storybook dungeon in a faraway castle, surrounded by fire-breathing beasts as real as the look on your face—as real as the space between us—and I can't get out.*

And I can't wake up from the dreams I've always had of you.

And I mean space, Julian—as if comets, moons, suns, stars are hurling through this typewriter between us . . .

Across the vacuum of a voyager named Phaedrus.

Julian, who are we? What do we mean to each other? In the vastness of our attraction, what's the matter? The gravity. The pull that holds us together—forever apart. . . .

Do we ever really touch, Julian? Even with naked flesh? Even with open pores? Even beneath mosquito nets! Or is there always a space between us—a furiously small expanse: a tiny layer of infinity—which must be the place where love is?

Which must be the place where death is.

Julian, how can we give Phaedrus that? How can we have it ourselves if he can see it? Don't you see that what he wants is the only thing we can't give, no matter how much he pays . . .

No matter how many paradoxes he pulls out of his pocket and shoves up our nose.

I want you to be my husband, Julian. I need you to be my wife. I must embrace that sense of family—of togetherness—of commitment—which Phaedrus is so quick to reject.

Even if it can't be legalized.

Even if it can't be sanctified.

It's what I grew up with, Julian. It's what my parents had. It's the only way I know to achieve something durable—something . . . predictable!

Julian, who was it who said if we look really hard at things we'll forget we're going to die? Who was it who said if love is the answer then we can't rephrase the question? Why does it make so much sense for me to still hope that you didn't know Phaedrus before, when I know that you'll know him again? Somewhere in the future of my past?

I just don't trust him, Julian. I just don't believe he will keep his hands off of us. In the end he will somehow make everything real—all of his fantasies—even if it's only through lies . . .

Even if it's only with his eyes.

Don't you see what will come to pass—a night of changing tenses? Before I'll know what to do? He'll be upon me like the drug. He'll be upon me just like you! It'll all seem to go so fast—the swirl of a hot tub; the motion of two men who look so much alike—who can, in fact, become mirrors. Throwing everything back. Giving everything so hard. Focusing it all on me. On three! On the thought that we'll be a group—like Anna and the man and the woman. Like Julian and Mary and Joseph. A couple plus one, again! Except, in this case, who will be the woman, Julian? And who will be the couple? Will it be you and me, in our tans? Or will it be Phaedrus and me, in our books? Or will it be you and Phaedrus, in your reflection? In your attraction?

Or is it the very thought that I can't figure it out which scares the shit out of me, Julian? Which makes it seem as if I have to get out of here before the curtain closes—before the act is final and Mexico is behind me forever!

Is that what I said? I don't know what I said. I was so numb, so high . . . So hot . . . So dizzy and wet with sweat . . . So that the words seemed to ooze out of me, as if directly from inside—through pores rather than lips—and yet I knew that Julian had understood. . . .

I could see him sweating back.

We were both so close to the fire.

We were almost touching knees.

I could feel the heat from his body.

And yet he seemed so far away, as if beyond some precipice—as if on a far-off mountaintop—hurling echoes back at me. . . .

"How foolish you are," he seemed to say. "How afraid of death you are," he seemed to say in a voice that was calmer yet much stronger than mine. "You look at life so hard that all you can see is death," he said. "A daily death," he called it, "and the harder you look at it the more it is bound to hurt. . . .

"Why does everything have to be so goddamned important to you?" he said. "Why does everything have to contain a metaphor?" he said. "Can't you just let things be what they are for a while? Can't you just let things take their own course without your turning them over for meaning—for detail to document your dying?

"I like you a lot, Robert," he seemed to say. "I even like the intensity you attribute to things. I even like the way you make me feel I'm your family—I'm in your heart—there's nothing you wouldn't do for me, nothing you wouldn't be for me. . . .

"How can I help but like that?" he said. "How can I help but respond to it—climb up a waterfall for it?

"But things just can't continue that way, Robert. Life just isn't that romantic. You just can't keep going deeper and deeper without eventually losing yourself. And then what have you got left for the other?

"Robert, I can't believe I'm making so much sense. I can't believe I'm finally saying it. You've been looking at me under a magnifying glass for so long that I couldn't help posing for you. I couldn't help becoming what you wanted to see. . . .

"Sure, I'd like things to be different. I'd love for us to get 'married.' It'd be great for us to have our own tiny Garden of Eden where we can plant what we want and make sure that it grows. Weed the rest of the world out. Turn every touch or word into a blossom or fragrance which is eternal.

"But it can't be like that, Robert—because I'm not you. I can't just go to a typewriter and make things happen. Instead I must go out and face a world that's already there—a life as I know it and must respond to it with each changing second, like that night you first followed me out of the gym . . . Down those streets . . . Toward that dirty bookstore . . . Into a shape that was already in your mind.

"Who did you think you were kidding, Robert? I knew all along you were behind me. I knew from the beginning what you were doing. That's why I became so helpless. That's why I finally agreed on Mexico. Because no one had ever made so much of me, Robert—so much of the *thought* of the touch of me, Robert.

"Well at last I have a little distance. Tonight I can see things more clearly, more calmly across this drug. . . . It's as if I have a life of my own now. It's as if all that you have given me—and all that you have attributed to me—has made me more. Has made me see that if I didn't lead you here to Phaedrus tonight, then you must have led me here to him. He must belong to a place in *your* mind. There must be something about him which you love, Robert—which may even be a part of your rejection of him—which has nothing to do with me. No matter what happens to us here tonight.

"Why must you be so quick to shut my world out—or to turn it into something else? A dark dungeon—an entire universe! Can't you just accept it—and accept me? And accept the fact that I don't want you to stay here, just as I don't want you to go? But rather I want you to want to stay—or want to want to go. And not with me, Robert—but with whatever this moment means to you.

"Who in the hell is Phaedrus anyway?" he said. "Why are you so goddamned afraid of him? Why do you feel you have to run away from him, carry him home in your imagination, turn him over in your mind—turn him into something you'll attach a meaning to? A reason for! Don't you see that by doing that you're only going to make him stronger, more immediate—more terrifying than anything he can possibly be *with* you?

"Robert, you've got everything backwards. You want everything for the wrong reasons. Whatever happens to us from this moment forward, or from any moment forward, cannot diminish what has passed—what already belongs to us. And yet we cannot take that past and freeze it like a photograph and call it the present—and allow it to frame the future—because it won't work. It won't expand our possibilities. It won't put off our deaths. It will only make our deaths seem more intimate, more pervading—more awesome to behold in each other.

"So let's embrace it now, Robert. Let's have sex *now,* Robert—in front of Phaedrus. Let's not even wait for that hot tub. Let's attack him, right here on his own ground—in front of dying embers. Let's let him know that we're in control—that even if we throw it at him he'll never be able to have what he really wants from us, which is our involvement with life. Something that changes with our every breath. Not something we can pull out of a book and pronounce in our minds, or pound through a typewriter and call it our own. And say it has life. And say it won't touch.

"We've got to *make* it touch, Robert. We've got to reach through these pages and fuck it, Robert. And fuck each other, Robert, as we reach out to him and hold on with our flesh. And pull him inside. And let him know who we are. And let him know how we feel. And let him know that he *can* have us, Robert—can have all of us, Robert; both the man and the woman of us, Robert—but that's all he'll ever have: that one grasp at our constant change. At our becoming new for each other through him!

"But quickly, Robert—you must make your mind up quickly. It's getting dark so fast in here. The fire is almost out. The caverns around us are deep. The books inside them are alive. The words are coming out of their paragraphs like vampires out of their coffins—like Phaedrus out of his trance—and so we must do something now, Robert. Even if it's dark and terrible.

"Even if it's bloody and violent.

"Because at least it will make Phaedrus real.

"At least it will give us a chance!"

Certainly that's what he said. It must have been something like that. *Even if he didn't speak a word. Even if he never said a thing.* The very shape of that room—of the shadows in his eyes, of the drugs in my mind—seemed to speak in Julian's voice of a planned death. Of a deliberately intended death. As if there were going to be a suicide.

As if there were going to be an execution.

At least that's how I saw it. I know that now. I can see that night so much more clearly now that I'm here in the future, at a desk which faces the darkness, putting the words back into his mouth. Actually hurling them like boomerangs across the wings of that angel dust and waiting for them to come back to me—turn in on me. Make me see now what I must have known instinctively back then: that to become like Julian would be to destroy everything I could possibly have with Julian. That I had no choice but to remain myself for his sake—for our sake.

Suddenly a calmness descended. Instantly I realized that even if they raped me they could never take away what was only mine to give. At that moment I smiled and accepted how easy it would be when I finally stood up and walked out of there, as if out of a movie—retreating in my mind to my sliding glass doors and exercising my prerogative as a woman to keep them out. I remember looking at Julian as if for the very last time, as if from very far away: speaking to him as if through the other end of a telephone which I at last decided to answer—which had been ringing for me all the time. I remember saying the words "I'm sorry," and then amending them to: "No, I'm not sorry—I'm sorrowful." And then saying in a deliberate whisper, only inches away from his ear, almost as if in prayer: "*But I'm not blaming anyone.*"

All the way home I was calm. I was so certain inside I was right. I didn't even try to justify it. I didn't even try to imagine what Phaedrus and Julian were doing back there without me. Suddenly my head was clear—the drug was gone. I just put my hands in my pockets and marched at a steady pace, heading through a section of the city with wide streets and spaces between every house—and flowers on every balcony—and I didn't feel at all intimidated. Not even by the shadows. In fact it was just the opposite. It had the echoes of a small neighborhood, of the safety with which I grew up—and for a moment I could imagine my mother sitting on the porch as my father mowed the lawn. Or as my brother headed home from school carrying the books of Sally next door (as I crouched in the bushes to surprise them, like something out of a Norman Rockwell painting). Don't ask me where the images came from—but suddenly Julian was a part of them. For a moment it was him crouching in the bushes with freckles on his face—not waiting for my brother and Sally, but waiting for me. A little-boy me! A grown-up kid walking down city streets with drugs in his mind—with Julian suddenly back in my heart as I wished I could make things different: as I tried to imagine a world where we could have grown up together, gone to the senior prom together, maybe even walked down an aisle hand in hand, arm in arm—like my brother and Sally. Like my mom and dad.

But how foolish it was to imagine such things. Julian was right when he said I was too damn romantic. Phaedrus was right when he said no one teaches us how to be gay. It was the weight of the word *straight*—of the *world* straight—that fell down on me now. That made me spit on the sidewalk as if in defiance of everything I had known before that moment. As I crossed a street and headed toward a more familiar section of the city I couldn't help thinking that even in Florida—in the sunshine state of Florida—the only moments I had known with men had been in the darkness of bars. Under the cover of night. Across the flatness of freeways. As if there had been something terribly, terribly wrong. . . .

But how was it different here? The entire city was like some gigantic bar. Everywhere you looked men were groping for men. Did it matter that it was out in the open—under the sun? Or under the stars? Is that what it means to be liberated?

Is that why I'm writing these words?

I remember making my way down a hill—turning a corner I had once turned behind Julian. The streets were more crowded now—our apartment much closer. The bars were just closing and I had no choice but to pass through the thick of it. At one corner two men were dressed completely in leather, both with beards and motorcycle caps—embracing passionately, almost furiously, as if pleasure had to hurt. As if only pain could protect. At another corner a man was standing alone, positioned strategically under an awning, not far away from a streetlight, so that only his face was in shadow—so that the rest of him was spectacularly in view. He had his thumbs tucked under his belt and his fingers stretched downward, giving emphasis to the immense bulge which beckoned from inside his pants. I remember hearing him grunt (or was it laugh?) as I kept cautiously close to the curb, scurrying past him like some animal—my eyes flashing backward, downward toward that bulge, as if it rather than he had the power to suddenly attack me. And yet still the calmness was inside me, even as I made my way through the throngs of men standing outside a bar called The Midnight Sun, which was just down the street from The Badlands. Which was around the corner from Toad Hall. Which wasn't too far away from The Moby Dick, which had a younger crowd. Or The Pendulum, which had a black crowd. Or The Twin Peaks, which had an older crowd. Or the donut shop, which stayed open all night—almost as a last resort. . . .

I remember elbowing my way through all of it, defying it to push back on me. Feeling in a way angry—or hurt. And yet still so amazingly calm, as if somehow in the eye of a hurricane. (As if the stillness itself spoke of danger.)

And yet still I didn't suspect a thing. I had no idea what was going on inside me. My refusal to think about Julian seemed to me logical—necessary. But by the time I got home and reached for my suitcase and started packing in front of the mirrors—determined to get out of there before Julian got back—I began to feel aggressive. I began to feel . . . horny! I looked at myself as if at somebody else and liked what I saw—and desired what I saw. Actually stepped toward the glass and reached with my hands and pressed with my lips and . . . that's when it happened.

Almost as if by design.

Almost as if Julian were right about metaphors—about how they always seemed to come back to me.

It was like discovering blood on my hands—or tears in my eyes. Or Digit in my duffel bag, just waiting to be delivered in a cab to a time when even the walls seemed to speak our sins. Except it was worse than that. It wasn't blood in my hand—but a splash of color, some epaulets, a button-down pocket: the shirt I had worn to Yelapa! The very contours of memory coming back to me, turning in on me: making me reach out slowly, with trembling fingers toward a moment, not a button—as if I were about to open a journal . . .

As if I were about to open an artery. . . .

Even before I saw it I remembered it. I remembered how I had turned around, saw Julian's horror across the deck. I remembered how I had reached for the camera and snapped the photo and put it in my mind long before it could ever develop in my pocket. I remembered how the bell had clanged, and Yelapa suddenly appeared, and all the tourists instantly tumbled toward our side of the boat—almost knocking us over. Forcing us against each other. Actually pressing us together as that photo was suddenly forgotten, isolated in time and a pocket—between the beat of two hearts: in the heat of our flesh—just waiting for a moment like this one.

That's when the calmness disappeared. That's when the drug came back in full force—bringing everything furiously into focus. That's when Digit suddenly rose up on hind legs, shrieking like a banshee—hissing as if at that photograph—tearing wildly across the carpet, out of the apartment, into the night.

It all seemed to happen in an instant, as if someone had pressed a button—as if Julian's telephone had screamed out a warning—and it took my mind several moments to accept the fact that that photograph was no longer a photograph, but something as terrible and transformed as what Phaedrus had become in his library. Immediately my mind went back there, trying to imagine what Julian looked like now—trying to imagine if Phaedrus and Julian had taken any more drugs, or taken off their clothes. But all I could see was how white Julian's face was—how wide his eyes were; how ghostly the whole thing appeared through a lens that was reaching too close: on paper that was crinkled and torn. The jungle in the background was so fantastically out of focus that it seemed more like an abstract painting—swirls of green licking like tongues at an image of Julian that had been faded by water and distorted by time—made to rhyme deliberately, almost too perfectly with a doodle Brian once drew of him. With a death Brian once knew of him!

I don't know how else to explain it. Suddenly I didn't trust anything. Somehow in that one moment—in that wild look on his face in my hand—I knew he would never come back to our apartment. I groped for him in my mind as if across some chasm that was unmeasurable—uncrossable as death. My first impulse was to race out of there, at least try to relocate Phaedrus' house—but the thought of all those solitary men on the streets between us was too much for me. They would be like peninsulas—extensions of the pavement rising up all around me—and I just couldn't deal with it. I wasn't even sure if I could find Phaedrus' house anyway. It had been so dark, and now I was so numb—so suddenly heavy. Pressing as if against weights. As if fighting the thought of Julian back. Pushing it harder and higher, up and actually out of some painted blue shell in my mind, as that photograph fell to the floor. As my body collapsed helplessly back into itself—back onto the bed. Back into the mirror. Far away from Julian. With no one to warm my insomnia. . . .

Eventually I must have slept—but only to reawaken very quickly, startled as if out of a dream, to find the lights still on—the sliding glass doors to the garden wide open—but my body too heavy to do anything about it. All night long it was like that—not really sleep; certainly not awake—but an endless drowsiness, a progression of half-images that didn't settle into slumber until dawn.

By the time I woke up it was late afternoon. Digit was nudging at me for some food. I was completely dressed and badly tangled in the sheets. Julian was nowhere in sight. The light outside was beginning to fade. I struggled to sit up on the bed and reach instinctively for a cigarette. I could hardly keep my eyes open as I lit it and sank back against a pillow and tried to piece the fragments back together. But they just wouldn't fit. No matter how hard I looked at them in my mind I just couldn't accept the fact that a hustler at a pool table would have a name like Phaedrus—or a house like the one he had led us to. For a moment I thought the whole thing had been planned—that at any moment Julian would walk out of the bathroom with a towel around his neck and a smile on his face and tell me it was some incredible joke. I opened my eyes to look toward the bathroom and was already cracking a smile of my own when I realized something was wrong. There were clothes strewn all around the bed, papers knocked off the desk; dishes broken everywhere around the counter as Julian's telephone lay among them, pulled entirely out by the cord. At first I was confused by the havoc—I thought I must still be in some dream. But then I found myself leaping up, realizing what I had done inside that drug—feeling my blood pump and my eyes bulge as I saw with horror that shirt I had worn to Yelapa. It had been torn wide open, ravaged as if it were flesh—strewn like viscera on the carpet in front of a mirror where Digit sat chewing on that photograph of Julian, gnawing away at his eyes, tearing open his heart: making me realize for the very first time what it would be like to have a life without Julian.

And so I decided to go back to The Arena. It seemed the only sensible thing to do. Maybe they would be there or maybe they wouldn't, but at least Brian would be there—at least I would have someone to try to explain things to. It made perfect sense to me then, as it does to me now from an even greater distance, that I had no choice but to forgive Julian—accept him on his terms. Allow him to have whatever he wanted from Phaedrus, or from the sailor—or from the old man or Mary or Joseph—as long as he came back to me. As long as whatever we had here in front of sliding glass doors would be ours alone—something to convince me that no matter how much it lacked (or maybe because of what it lacked) it had something very special to give. Something to support me in my life.

That's exactly the way I would say it. I had a whole speech made up in my mind. I rehearsed it out loud as I fed the cat and vacuumed the carpet as if erasing the evidence of some crime. I wanted everything to be as close as possible to the night when Julian first arrived here. I even showered and shaved and put on the same plaid shirt I had worn the night I had followed him out of the gym. I told myself that he might not remember it, but on some instinctive level he might feel it—and know how much I needed him back with me. The last thing I did before I left the apartment was go out to the garden and pick some calla lilies and arrange them on the table by the door, so they would be the very first thing he would see when he finally arrived back home—as if nature itself would be rejoicing.

But was I being foolish? Was I making myself out to be too much of a romantic? Was it wrong for me to admit how much I was willing to do for him? Yes, I can see now it's true that I was the woman of our relationship—at least on that night when I thought I had lost him. When I found Digit devouring what little I had left of him! I remember racing into The Arena as if in skirts that rubbed everybody the wrong way. Even Brian looked at me as if at someone who just didn't belong there. It was obvious from the way I moved through the crowd and ignored all the eyes that I had a weakness for only one person. I didn't even order a drink. I just headed for the pool table in the back of the bar knowing that if Julian were there then that's where he'd be. And if he weren't then I would wait for him—wait all night if necessary. And if he never showed up then I would flag down a cab and be driven through that section of town where I thought Phaedrus lived—where I hoped that I'd find them. But how useless it seemed to locate that house when I thought of that drug which had driven me into a violence I could hardly remember. If it had done that to me—if it had caused me to ransack my own home without my even knowing it—then God knows what it might have done to Julian and Phaedrus.

Suddenly I imagined the worst. I imagined headlines screaming the news of Julian's death. I remembered descriptions I had read of the mad doodler, believed to be a homosexual himself—blond, about six-one, who always picked his victims up in bars. Autopsies revealed the one similarity among all the victims—a total of six so far—(besides the fact they had been sexually mutilated)—was the high concentration of drugs in their blood. And one article noted that all of them had been found with a large denomination, usually a fifty- or one-hundred-dollar bill in their pocket.

I give you such detail only to point out how my mind works sometimes. As I pushed my way through the last wall of men my hands were trembling. As I neared the pool table and the possibility of Julian I became convinced that Phaedrus fit perfectly the description of the mad doodler—right down to his fifty-dollar bill. Suddenly that photo I had taken in Mexico seemed a portent of something terrible which already had happened: the death mask of Julian in some city morgue. I knocked over one man's drink and tripped over the feet of another as I finally stumbled like a drunk into the smoke-filled clearing surrounding the pool table and saw immediately what I was looking for—Phaedrus leaning over the pool table.

Phaedrus without Julian.

Phaedrus looking once again young and sexy and blond and . . . somehow rejuvenated, like a vampire after drinking blood.

The images may sound farfetched but the reality was too much a part of me to waste any time.

I leaped at him—lunged at him before he could make his shot—knocking him over and landing on top of him in a tangle of flesh which happened too fast for anybody to make much sense out of.

All those perfectly groomed men who had been watching him—probably desiring him—were too stunned to do anything but watch as that cue stick in his hands suddenly struck my nose and sent blood spurting everywhere on Phaedrus' shirt—on his face and neck and hands—as my head struck the side of the pool table.

As his arms instantly overwhelmed me.

As his entire body was suddenly on top of me, pressing down on me, as if sexually, and then . . . he erupted furiously into a laugh.

He leaned forward as if to lick my blood.

He was about to kiss me, or speak to me about Julian—tell me something awful; tell me what I had come to hear—when . . . suddenly Brian appeared.

When . . . suddenly Julian appeared.

It all seemed to happen at once.

Apparently he had been in the bathroom.

Apparently they were still together.

But before Brian could take things in hand Julian came to the rescue.

He peeled Phaedrus off of me.

He helped me to my feet.

He reached for his handkerchief and wiped off the blood and . . . then it happened.

It happened like it happened when I saw him in that photograph.

His face seemed so ghostly, his eyes so . . . intense.

As if fueled by some drug.

As if that's why he had been in the bathroom—for a hit of cocaine.

"Robert," he said as everyone listened—as even the smoke seemed to freeze in midair—but that's all he said.

I had never seen him so beautiful—so physically beautiful as he looked back at me, transformed by the pallor on his face and the dim glow of the bar: looking as smooth and innocent and soft and perfect as a child, but his voice being just the opposite—colder, harder, more frightened (yes, frightened!) than I had ever heard it. . . .

"Go home, Robert," he said very slowly, pronouncing each word as if it were a sentence—a verdict that was irrevocable: unpardonable.

"Get out of here, Robert," he said somewhat louder, giving emphasis to my name—too much weight to one end of a remark that seemed to tumble downward like his eyes.

"I don't want to hurt you, Robert!" he suddenly shouted, not so much out of anger—but as if to warn me of some danger. "I can't hurt you, Robert! Not you, Robert! Not anymore, Robert! You're not real, Robert!"

And then he was crying—pleading. Shouting above the music. Suddenly grabbing me by my shoulders and shaking me—squeezing me as if he really hated me. *"Go home, Robert! Get out of here, Robert! Get back to your own life, Robert!"* Slurring his words. Dripping saliva down his chin. A spot of my blood on his shirt—another on his pants. His eyes so wide and blue and fiery. His voice so loud and hard, echoing as if through streets as the tears continued in his eyes. As the tears came to my eyes, too—knowing there was nothing I could do in front of all these men. Knowing that anything I might say would only irritate him—maybe provoke him; certainly embarrass him. . . .

So finally, finally I reached out and touched his trembling lips as if to quiet him—as if to tell him with one finger what I could never say with words: that it was the city which had conspired against us. Then I turned around and headed calmly toward the door, ignoring the eyes of Brian, keeping my head bowed as if in prayer so the other men wouldn't see the tears in my eyes: the despair of knowing that Julian and Phaedrus would go home together, climb into a hot tub together, take some more drugs together, perhaps even remain together in front of mirrors or inside the borders I could never again return to—except of course through memory. As if the visa to understanding Julian lay somewhere in the past: in the mirror of his father's sex—on the quicksilver between life and death—or maybe inside that painted blue shell of thought, with its chambers now closing upon me, like the lid of a coffin descending, as I stepped quietly into the night . . .

Wounded in more than my sex. . . .

• • •

I can see now what I have been doing from the very beginning—recording experiences not in the order in which they took place, for that is history; but in the order in which they first became significant for me, which is a history of my heart. That journal I had written in one day, for example—starting at a glass-topped table and ending at an outdoor café—came out of me long after that encounter with Phaedrus: and yet Phaedrus was never mentioned in it. Why, I ask myself now, did I expunge him as if deliberately from the perspective of Julian I was giving you at the time? Should I have let you know in one fell swoop that it was not the first time Julian had walked out on me—just as I must now let you know that I had no choice but to accept him back after Phaedrus? Writing, it seems, is never a voyage into the future. . . .

And so I must go back now, go back as if for the very last time to the beginning of the end—to the very last time Julian moved out on me, this time taking his telephone with him. And yet even then it wasn't over because still he kept coming back, sometimes at weird hours of the night, sometimes in the very early morning with a bottle of Cold Duck he had bought at the all-night liquor store, pressing it against my cheek and waking me up to the chill of a truth still inside me: that I was happy to have him hold on. That I insisted he keep his own keys.

It didn't matter that he was at the end of his high, heavy after a long night of sex. It didn't matter that his breath sometimes smelled, and his body was steeped in the odor which defined him. I took him in and drank his wine and was happy just to have him lie there, hold on to me, fall asleep in the same bed I was just waking up from. There was something very intimate—almost sexual—about watching him fall asleep in the same sheets, surrendering as if to my dreams, as the coffee brewed on the stove. . . .

And then one morning I heard a flute outside our window. I was half asleep but still holding on to the thought of Julian beside me. I hadn't seen him for over a week and then suddenly he was there: appearing with the earliest light and slipping silently between my sheets. It was happening more and more like that: without the Cold Duck, without the wake-up smile—without any desire for sex. And yet still I was happy for what I had. It felt so good to have him pressing naked against me, his breath so heavy against the back of my neck as he reached out with one arm, as if with the last remnant of consciousness to pull me into his sleep: to commit himself to my keep. I couldn't help but respond to it—become erect for it. Reach with my own hand to my own sex for it. And then I heard that flute. . . .

I didn't even bother to dress. I stumbled naked to my sliding glass doors. Digit was at my heels. The morning light had an eerie quality—an almost ghostly quality, as if it were appearing everywhere at once rather than coming from a certain direction. It was February, I remember, because my primroses were making their winter appearance: and my pine tree was shedding its cones. And there were no signs of snails—no silvery trails left by those slippery creatures who inhabited only the night. As I slid open the glass Digit leaped quickly ahead, prancing across the baby tears and up the fence where suddenly he froze, his cat eyes narrowing—his sleek neck stretching upward as he searched that immense pine tree as if for some exotic bird.

But that's where reality ends. Everything else happened as if in some dream. The music of that flute seemed to contain every color imaginable—like light in a prism. There was no way for me to tell where it was coming from. I took one step after another, forgetting I was naked—forgetting I was in the backyard of some city block where any neighbor's eyes might be upon me. Suddenly my garden became a mythological forest—and Digit some transfigured god who had inhabited that shape to deceive me. And when I looked up: looked high through the boughs of that pine tree and saw him sitting there, as if balanced on the branches, that flute to his lips, that wavy blond hair falling to one side, I was certain it was an apparition: some angel or goat-boy of God, who had been sent to deliver me from Julian. . . .

And then his eyes turned upon me, looking down through the needles of pine, but the flute was still to his lips. He was speaking to me as if through his notes. They were fluttering in the air all around me. They were landing like calendar pages on the ground. I remember picking one up to examine it—to read it as if it were words. It told me to step out in the open.

It said he was waiting to see.

And that's where the fantasy ended—or maybe really began. I stepped out from under that tree to find him sitting on a tiny balcony, at the corner of the house next to Brian's—leaning against a railing, one leg dangling freely in air, the other propped up against the building, wearing nothing but gray sweatpants which were bunched high over his calves but stretched tightly to the curves of his ass—as if deforming his lower body. Giving it the shape of something with hooves.

But neither of us spoke a word. And I wasn't a bit embarrassed to be naked. It seemed somehow to fit perfectly into the scheme of things—my dream of things. . . . I just stood there watching and listening, loving the way his eyes like his music seemed to drink me up, take me inside—actually move through me like his breath moved through that flute: as if I were some instrument of his enchantment. As if his fingers were plugging up my holes, dancing over my body. . . .

And so right away I retreated inside, closing the glass doors behind me. Locked between them and the mirrors. Looking at Julian asleep. Not even wanting to know that man's name—or where he had come from. Not wanting to dispel the magic—the fantasy in my own backyard. It had been months since I had felt so light, so ethereal: so much like when I first descended as if by parachute on San Francisco—and I loved it that way. I wanted that magic back in my life. It made me look at Julian as if for the first time. It helped me to see him with a distance I had never allowed myself before. It was as if that flute had suddenly drawn a line across my life—like a thirtieth birthday; like a father's death—transporting me into a new awareness of loss as the meaning of life. Of acceptance as the only salvation.

It was impossible to shut it out completely. The notes seemed to leak through the glass. They were distant, muted—like Julian in his sleep; like a memory in my mind. They accompanied me like the soundtrack to a movie as I made my way to his bed, as I had in Puerto Vallarta—after the maid had knocked at our door with a smile on her face and towels in her hand. "*Buenas tardes,*" she had said as I returned to Julian naked on the bed, that fan spinning above his head, those waves crashing outside the window off our balcony as I couldn't help watching him—the line of his tan. His tantalizing manhood. A mosquito bite on his leg as he slept so deeply, so steeply. . . .

Except this time there was no tan. It had been months since our return from Mexico. It had been nearly six weeks since he had moved out with his telephone and not given any explanation for where he was living. Of course I had seen him scores of times at the gym, pumping away more furiously than ever. And heaven knows how many times he had showed up here in the middle of the night, or in the middle of the afternoon—always unannounced, always with some drug—allowing me to take out that tiny tape recorder as we sat in the garden and mellowed with the light: and talked about his past as it became increasingly apparent that Julian was opening up to me, becoming more comfortable with me—speaking to a friend as he could never have spoken to a lover about the time he saw his father masturbating. Or about the time he actually put his hand on his father's penis. . . .

"I don't remember how old I was," he said. "I might even have been in high school, but for some reason the time escapes me. All I know is my father was sleeping in the afternoon. He had some kind of important meeting that night. He was sleeping in his underwear and the blanket had been tossed aside. I looked at him, at the outline in his underpants, at his white, almost hairless legs. He was snoring. I knew he was sound asleep. I could hear my mother downstairs washing dishes. The phone rang in the distance. My father turned over on one side. I stepped closer, looking at him for a long time, maybe as long as five minutes, looking between his legs, wondering, wondering. Did I really come from that? Is it possible? I could hear my mother's voice on the telephone, discussing a recipe for brownies. It seemed as if she were a million miles away. The snoring continued. That, too, seemed a million miles away. I reached out slowly, very slowly, my hand trembling. It was shaking so badly that I had to pull it back, hold it with my other hand. I was breathing deeply, yet trying not to make any noise, trying not to disturb this sleeping man I called 'father.' 'Our Father who art in Heaven ...' Strange, but that's what went through my mind at the time. 'Our Father who art in Heaven, hallowed be thy ...' The mind-words came involuntarily. '... Thy Kingdom come, Thy will be done ...' My fingers reached the soft cotton of his underwear. There was a stain. I remember how it disgusted me for some reason. But still I touched, ever so gently—touched and rubbed and felt and listened to my heart beating a thousand times a minute. 'Give us this day our daily bread, and forgive us our ...' I thought the beating of my heart might wake him up, it was so loud. Yet my hand was calmer now, calm as it rested on his sleeping penis, calm as it slid into the crack of his underwear, the opening where he pissed ... 'Our father who art in bed ...' I tried to move my hand farther, but it wouldn't go. I touched the cloth, touched the outline, but couldn't touch the flesh. '... Hallowed be thy ... thy ...' Suddenly the snoring stopped. He didn't move, but the snoring stopped! I was afraid to move my hand, afraid to wake him up. Afraid that he might already be awake, feeling the feel of me. 'Our Father, my father ... thy kingdom ... come ... come ...' Suddenly I had no choice but to jerk my hand away, quickly away, in one fast movement—just yanking it and holding it to my chest, hoping for dear life that he wasn't awake as my mother called from downstairs: 'Julian! Julian!' I remember I took giant steps. I remember my heart was still racing. I remember I went to my room, my next-door room, then heard the snoring again ... again, thank God! Then I started downstairs as my heart slowed down a bit—as the snoring went on—as I took a deep breath and said: 'Amen . . .' And thought: 'A man . . .' as I returned to my mother and accepted the bowl she had given me to lick from the brownies. Applying the same finger I had applied to my father's sex. Bringing it deliberately to my mouth as I looked at my mother with the full realization that this was the beginning—the beginning of whatever was ahead. . . .

"Do you see what I mean?" he had said, sitting in the sunshine of my garden, pausing to hand me the joint, leaning very close as his face seemed to darken and even clouds seemed to pass overhead. "Does it explain how I moved through that world as if on secrets that would somehow define me—at least give me some kind of identity! Everything else had limits, borders, commandments—restraints built implicitly into it. The one place I could go with freedom—the only place I could go with the sureness of being an adult—was into my own head. Into my father's bed!"

I remember looking at Julian as if something were suddenly very wrong—out of focus. I remember seeing his sleeping form as I had seen his eyes in the garden—as I had seen Phaedrus looking back at me in the firelight: with pain, revulsion; as if he were very old, lashing back much too late. For the first time I began to distrust everything Julian had said to me—all those nights he had crawled in bed with me. Even his body seemed to speak of lies that could not be softened through the gauze of mosquito nets. I remember looking at it, actually probing at that body as if to perform an autopsy. All those drugs he had taken night after night since the moment he had moved out of here were at last taking their toll. I could see heavy bags under his eyes, large bruises on his thighs. And not only had his skin lost its tan from Mexico, but it actually seemed white, bleached—stretched tightly like cellophane over a container. And yet still his muscles were very strong—pumped fuller than ever from the even more elaborate workouts he had imposed on himself, as if to make up for the drugs. The trouble was those muscles were now too big—out of proportion to his wrists and ankles and head. And as he lay there in my bed, crouched in a semifetal position, his chest muscles bloated like breasts, his thick penis tucked somewhere inside the folds of his legs—his lips so hollow; his hair so matted and long—he looked for all practical purposes like an anomaly: neither man nor woman, but some creature battered and broken in its sex.

But what drove me to an even deeper despair was the sound of that flute outside my window, as transparent as Julian's skin—as vacuous as his words inside my tape recorder: the perfect accompaniment to this moment of introspection that had traveled over such a distance. It seemed so far away—and yet so suddenly clear that everything had changed; that my priorities like Julian's body had been completely rearranged since that night he had appeared at the café, actually stepping into my words as if inside the pages of some book. (I remember how passionately we had embraced in the shadows—how frantically we had grabbed like children at the very images I had just been writing about.) But even that moment, like the moment he had come back to me after a full week with Phaedrus—with flowers in his hand; with Quaaludes in his pocket—was somehow robbed of all joy by the disgust I suddenly felt toward myself for always believing at such moments that we were starting anew: blossoming into love—accepting each other's forgiveness—when in truth our relationship was dying slowly, of a twisted sort of dependency that was grounded more in fear; that that flute had made me hear!

I don't know how else to explain it. I just know I remained there for hours, studying Julian naked in his sleep like some specimen in a jar—my repulsion as great as my attraction as the morning gave way to afternoon and the sunlight changed directions in my garden. (I'm not even sure when that flute ceased its serenade; I just know at one point it was over, like my feelings of desire for his flesh.) And yet I couldn't help going back, spiraling through my entire life with Julian: all the way to Mexico; back inside a peek machine—a camera!—a generator!—that tape recorder which now seemed to be the final container: the ultimate inhabiter of the only thing I had left with Julian—words!

I was like some madman trying to piece the whole thing together. First I would play part of a tape, then read part of my journal. Then I would take out that album of Mexico—the one I had put together during that "golden period" just after our return. Then after a few pages I would get fidgety, anxious—make myself a cup of coffee. Ignore Julian on the bed. Finally put on some pants and head out to the garden and look up to that empty balcony or fuss over my primroses and wonder whether Brian was home. And wonder whether any of this was really happening. And wonder whether even Phaedrus in my head like the muse on that balcony had been part of some elaborate fiction—some game-plan in my imagination for arriving at the darkest night I had ever had with Julian.

And then it came back to me—the image of Julian on that final night: grabbing a knife and holding it in front of his face and looking me hard in the eyes, then reaching with massive fingers toward that telephone cord which he severed with the violence of a jugular vein. (It was probably the last truly sexual moment I had had with Julian.) I remember how angry he had been that I had once again brought up Phaedrus—used him as a reference point in time—and that's how the whole thing had started. "Can't you just forget it!" he had screamed at me. "Do you have to keep erecting memorials to that one missing week in our lives!" But in truth this argument had been going on for a long time—probably since the moment he had had his telephone put back in—and so neither of us was very surprised and yet both of us quite visibly shaken when Julian finally severed that cord as if it were umbilical and stormed with his hatred toward the door. "You may accuse me of having left you," were his final words, spoken over his shoulder as if from very far away—as if over some massive barrier of stone—"but I accuse you of wanting me gone!"

But he came back—back as he always came back. Back in the early morning—or back in the middle of the afternoon. Or back on a day like that day when I walked as if on tiptoes from my garden to my apartment, from my winter primroses to that summer album of dreams so carefully arranged and labeled. I remember looking at those pages as if through binoculars—or as if through some tiny screen of a peek machine where I could actually see it going on. There was one photo that Pamela had taken of Dianne mounted on our shoulders, stacked as if on top of a pyramid, trying to keep her balance, when one strap of her bikini snapped and her tit burst loose and as she tried to contain it we all went tumbling to the sand. That photo had captured it perfectly—the burst of flesh, the bulging of eyes; the flexing of one of Julian's enormously tanned thighs as he attempted to keep us all from colliding. But of course he couldn't, and so there was an explosion of laughter that echoed again as it did back then at the thought of how it had happened—at the sight of it happening again. . . .

For a moment I thought I had woken up Julian. He turned over on one side and muttered something indistinguishable, then reached for a pillow and embraced it as if it were a person. I remember dropping the scrapbook and stepping very close and thinking under my breath: No, don't wake up, Julian—not yet; just give me a little more time. For the first time since I had known him I felt . . . intruded upon. It was a feeling so new that it startled me—and then irritated me. Here I was, about to arrive at something in my mind: some conclusion that could come with a little more distance—with a few more images—and then his presence was suddenly upon me. Even the few breaths he took as he stirred inside that pillow without returning to consciousness were enough to pull like gravity: to awaken something I couldn't control—some gnawing persistence of ... passion.

How I suddenly hated it—hated myself for feeling it—looked at that battered body as if for excuses not to like it. How I wanted to find something tangible, some concrete evidence—say needle marks instead of mosquito bites—anything that would give me the proof I needed for kicking him out of my apartment: for taking away his keys. It was as if that album I had just been looking at had brought everything into focus: had made me see that what Julian was holding on to—that what he kept coming back to—was not only what I had created; but what I had arranged, labeled and defined—mounted as deliberately as mirrors on my wall. Yes, he did love what I had to give—the comfort of sheets; the warmth of acceptance—but more than anything he loved my power to forgive: to listen to all those crimes of his childhood as if I could somehow absolve him as an adult, grant grace to his existence as a hustler.

By the time Julian woke up it seemed clear I had somehow outgrown him—outlived him. It was as if that day had been a spaceship and I had traveled light-years in only hours. I remember how cranky and groggy he seemed as he made his way to my bathroom and threw up in the toilet. It was now nearly dark—he had slept a full twelve hours—and yet his body seemed heavier and those bags under his eyes much bigger than I had ever noticed before. Somehow they reminded me of Phaedrus in the library—so young, and yet so old. Or that old man I had seen through a panel of glass: so crippled he could barely get to his feet until he started nurturing himself on the sexual juices of Julian. In a way these two men seemed to turn on me from the ends of a spectrum—as if from directly opposite chambers on the spiral of my experience of Julian: to actually look at me with recognition and then start yelling as if through glass, waving frantically as if to warn me of some approaching danger.

But of course it is easy for me to put it that way now that it is over—now that the mirrors are gone and I've got no one to blame but myself (and no one to be with but you). It has been so long since that night, and yet still it keeps coming back like a bad reflection—distorted, rearranged; as if it happened too fast to keep track of. I remember telling the police it was suicide—suicide like his father—but they kept asking me to remain calm, not to touch anything: just to sit quietly at the table by the door. So I picked up the cat and started stroking its back, concentrating really hard on the fur, when one officer asked me how it was Julian had ended up in the garden—how his head had managed to strike the jagged border of bricks surrounding my calla lilies. But all I could say was "the muse . . . the music! . . ."—over and over again: too numb to make any sense; too stunned even to be embarrassed when one of them found a jar of Vaseline like an icon behind the bed, with some of Julian's blond hairs still stuck to it. . . .

When Julian came out of the bathroom he didn't speak a word. The first thing he did was pour himself a drink—bourbon in an orange-juice glass: no ice, no water. He seemed blinded by the fluorescent light over the sink and yet made no attempt to darken it. Everything that happened that night—even the way the bourbon fell out of the bottle—seemed to be in slow motion. The only acknowledgment he gave me was a slight nod of the head as he lifted his glass and then closed both eyes, either in pain or ecstasy. Then he went mechanically about the business of finding his clothes—locating a sock here, his pants there; returning periodically to the counter for another sip of bourbon but never saying a word as he got dressed. It seemed to me as if he already knew what was in my mind. I could tell by the way he paused at one point with a shoe in his hand and looked at me as if we were playing some kind of game—seeing who would speak the first word. Wondering what that first word would be. Waiting for it to exit a mouth and enter the apartment as if on legs that would march between us, with the power to wreak havoc or happiness. . . .

At least that's how my mind interpreted it. Suddenly I found myself hating the smug expression on Julian's face. Somehow I despised the way he walked to my desk and picked up the tape recorder and pressed the "record" button—then reached for his jacket and pulled out a joint with the certainty it would draw a response from me. It was as if he had everything planned step by step, defying me to make real what was in my mind so he could have an excuse to play it back: blame me for whatever would happen—accuse my love or my fear or my guilt, and somehow make the whole thing look like murder. . . .

But how can I say for sure? How can I know what was going on inside of Julian when I was so wrapped up in myself? Maybe he just wanted to talk some more about his father. Maybe he just wanted to smoke that joint and share some thoughts he might never have shared with another? Maybe that look on his face was really one of love—of Julian's kind of love—(of Julian's way of showing love)—and so maybe I was missing the opportunity of a lifetime. Maybe that would have been the moment of moments when Julian would have come back to me, really held on to me—even repented his ways for me. (Isn't that what every woman dreams of—having a love so strong it could change the shape of the world?)

The trouble was that's how it always happened. Every time was supposed to be the time Julian would be strong for me—strong in his grasp of me. How could I wait around any longer? How could I hope any harder? Usually when I looked at Julian I would see everything we might one day become—but suddenly I was seeing everything we'd never be. Suddenly I looked across that tiny apartment at his hollow eyes and shrunken head and saw something I couldn't escape: my own life. Some inscrutable void as monstrous as the need for happiness. . . .

Don't you see it was me not him I was attacking inside that

tape recorder? Don't you see it was *my* life I was calling into question, hurling into doubt? It was as if that flute outside my window had joined the beat inside my heart to weave a cocoon that instantly numbed me, insulated me like a drug—then made me react as if with withdrawal symptoms to the sexual oppression of Julian. I know it sounds dramatic but it was real—real as the image of Brian across the garden. Real as that joint Julian put to a match and took inside his lungs as I saw Brian getting dressed for work, over Julian's shoulder—beyond our sliding glass doors—as a voice suddenly erupted from inside me . . .

"Angel dust!" I cried out so loud, with such fury at my recognition of that smell—of knowing that Julian was doing it against me—that for a moment I thought Brian had heard it. (Later he would explain to authorities that he was late for work; that he had heard something like a shout and looked toward our apartment and saw us facing each other across the counter but didn't really have the time to investigate.) It was now completely dark outside. I knew that flute was gone. I knew there was no moon. I wanted Brian somehow to come to my rescue and save me from my words, but . . . how could he? He was no longer a part of my life. I had excluded everybody. I had become more desperate than Desire, more perverse even than Phaedrus, willing to pay with my very soul—and the shape of my life—the price of having loved Julian. . . .

It became clear in that one enormous shout (and in the way Julian looked back at me as if sexually aroused) that I could have been standing on some streetcorner. At least that's how I saw it. My words didn't seem to make any difference. It was my fury which Julian suddenly responded to. I remember telling him I was tired if not terrified of the way he kept coming back day after day, sometimes in the middle of the night—always with some new drug, as if to die a little bit more in front of me. But still my message had no effect. He just kept smiling, leering—then reaching toward his crotch. Looking younger than I had ever seen him. Stepping very slowly around the counter, as if through a time warp. Keeping his eyes on mine as he had that night we first arrived here, delivered from a cab as if from a womb, with that blank notebook still in my hand. . . .

How excited Julian had been that night. Everything had happened as if inside his ultimate sexual fantasy. First the streets, then that peek machine. Me following him, then him turning on me. Mirrors, shadows, curtains, darkness—and then the cab. It's what Julian loved. Later he would tell me he had never been more intrigued, especially when the cab driver turned on us and called me: "the writer!"—as if I fit into a category like: "the sailor!"

"But what really blew me away," Julian would say much later in our relationship, on an afternoon in the sunshine with a tape recorder, "was when we walked into your apartment. It wasn't at all what I imagined. After what had happened that night on the streets I was expecting something more severe. Maybe leather. Certainly mirrors! But instead I found . . . calla lilies on the table. And Digit in your bed. And all those papers piled around your typewriter as if . . . something were really going on here.

"Everybody in this business has mirrors," he said. "Even the old people. I've never yet been to a place that didn't have a lot of them, and at least one fairly close to the bed. . . .

"But you—you . . . puzzled me. I didn't really know what was happening. You seemed to know so much about what you were doing in that porno bookshop, but then . . . when we got to your apartment . . . you were like some child stumbling all over itself. Asking me would I like this to drink, would I like that on the stereo. Would I like to step out in the garden and have a look at the fuchsias. I couldn't believe you were the same person. I thought maybe you had somehow pulled a switch on me, yanked some twin brother out of the closet when I had my back turned. Honest to God, you were that different—and that deceptive.

"And then we touched," Julian said that day in the sun. "And then we made love without any mirrors," he said, "and I could feel your body responding as if aching for my sex. Holding on so hard with your pleasure that . . . it hurt. It hurt me, too! It inhabited the both of us—made me want to take you over, own you, stay inside you all night—but the next thing I knew we were in Mexico . . .

"And then we were home . . .

"And then we met Phaedrus . . .

"And then I came back to you . . .

"And now we are . . . *here*," Julian said. "At the moment when it all comes together."

Julian was very stoned. It was obvious the angel dust was coming on quickly. He stepped toward me in slow motion, spoke only with his eyes, yet got closer and closer with such raw force—with such brute determination—as if saying: "See, I've still got the power of sex over you!"

What happened next was furious. Everything seemed to go everywhere at once, as if in a rape—and yet still in slow motion. He was upon me and I pushed him back. I told him no—and I meant it. I told him to get off of me, to get away from me—it just wouldn't work anymore. But still he refused to listen. He couldn't accept the fact that I would reject his body. He kept coming at me without saying a word, without having said a word since he woke up: just sucking on that joint and stepping again and again toward the certainty of my giving in to him. But I wouldn't. I didn't care that his eyes seemed to mock me, that his powerful arms seemed to play games with me. He bounced me against the refrigerator and I knocked him against the counter. The joint fell out of his hand. Immediately I retrieved it and stuffed it down the sink before he could stop me. He was wild with anger, suddenly turning on me with real venom. But this time I ducked and he went slamming into the sink, hitting his head on one of the cupboards, falling back against the refrigerator and knocking off one of those photos of Digit in a sombrero. And that's when it happened.

Something inside him seemed to crack.

That photo went swirling to the floor at Julian's feet.

He looked at it as if he had lost a part of himself—some organ or limb, or some long-remembered sin of his childhood.

He seemed so confused, so . . . out of focus. For a moment I thought he was going to cry. . . .

For a moment I thought he was some little kid with a bruised knee about to run home for a kiss from his mother.

But then I saw something darker, something much more determined in the way Julian lifted his eyes and refused to acknowledge the bump on his forehead as he crossed that small room toward his jacket. I don't know what it was that angered me so much but suddenly I wanted to yell at him—accuse him with his own body of never having loved. "If only you could see yourself!" I wanted to shout. "If only you could see what a pathetic caricature you've become of yourself!" But Julian wouldn't allow this indignity. Before the words could form on my lips he reached inside his jacket and pulled out a cellophane bag of angel dust—and the look on his face spoke it all. It told me I better not touch him. It said in his own time he'd leave.

At first I thought he was going to roll another joint and smoke it as a final act of defiance. I decided I had no choice but to accept it. But I decided he better give me my keys back—or I would change all the locks on the door. I told him as much in a voice as calm as I could make it, controlled as if by thermostat. But he just looked at me and smiled as if to say he knew something I didn't. Then, before I could stop him—before I could barely comprehend what was happening—he licked his middle three fingers and dipped them into the angel dust and brought them to his lips, his gums, his tongue, his nose—licking and dipping and rubbing and smiling and saying something about his father. Something about how he hadn't shot himself into a mirror at all, but into something much darker—something . . . much more sexual! That was the word Julian used and suddenly it frightened me—not just the sound of it, but the shape of it in Julian's eyes. The way he took that angel dust by the fingersful and thrust it into his nose. Inhaling as hard as he could. Spilling it all over his chin. Rubbing some more on his lips. Then laughing when I suddenly charged him, tried to knock it out of his hand, but instead tripped into the desk and knocked off the tape recorder and heard it slam against the floor, snap completely into silence, as if that had been the moment of Julian's death.

By the time I wrestled that bag out of his hand his lips were already blue. The blood vessels around his nose were bursting into tiny red blotches. His eyes had withdrawn into two dark pinpoints as the bags beneath them continued to swell. His entire face was distorted, puffed beyond recognition, and I could tell even his hands were numb as he tried to push himself up off the carpet. My first impulse was to race to the telephone and call for help but before I could get there he had heard something. He was standing up and turning his head and trying to find it. I looked at him looking in every direction and then walking squarely into the mirror. I ran to stop him but it was too late. He fell back against me, knocked me down, but somehow managed to stay on his feet. And that's when I heard it, too.

It was coming from out in the garden.

It was summoning as it had that morning.

It was so awful—and yet so beautiful.

Julian seemed to respond to it as if to a voice from his past.

"Yes," he said out loud, so perfectly lucid—so suddenly in control of everything that was about to happen. "Yes, I know—I know."

And that's what made it so scary—the involvement he had with that flute. The way he walked so numbly out into the garden and raised his arms as if in homage to the darkness, then embraced himself as if it were an act of sex. What could I do but watch from the doorway—watch him spinning around and around as if on some dance floor? Suddenly I no longer existed—no longer had ever existed! No longer could ever again exist for Julian except through the kind of death that happens only with words, once you have made them your own. . . .

Isn't that why I came back here in the first place: to tell you how awful it was? How predictable it should have been!

Isn't that what I was expecting from the sailor tonight: an excuse for it—a way of freeing myself from the guilt for it!

It was as if Julian's death were the most shameful sexual act he could possibly have performed—*and I just couldn't keep from watching it.*

I knew I should have gotten to the telephone or cried out for help, but it seemed to me in those few moments before he fell as if he were . . . not speaking to me, but . . . performing for me. Calling like that flute to me, and . . . I couldn't take my eyes off him.

(But who am I kidding? Certainly not the police! They keep coming around asking questions, searching for a misplaced detail, and in a way their suspicions are right: I did in a sense allow it. I could have prevented Julian from losing his balance, hitting the ground—if only I had known. But still that's not how he died. It's what happened after that fall that was so terrible: that made me run to him like a whore, as if summoned by a telephone to participate—to acknowledge that flute as a real call to Julian's destiny!)

He landed flat on his back with his head on the bricks, his eyes wide open. The boughs of the pine tree above him. The long shadows streaming across the garden—the light like a lantern that was our apartment. He was so perfectly still. . . .

He was lying there almost with a smile, hardly breathing, looking so much at last at rest—his distorted face somehow transformed by the shadows into a look of anticipation. As if he had just caught someone's eye on the street. . . .

The calla lilies had not yet blossomed, but their thick stems and huge leaves were exploding out of the ground near Julian's face—as if already planted at the base of some tombstone to deliver his memory to the sunlight. . . .

"Julian," I whispered very softly, falling to my knees, trying to ignore the sounds of the flute, trying to see his face through the shadows and . . . at least make him blink his eyes. "Julian, can you hear me?"

But he didn't blink his eyes. He didn't move at all. For a moment I thought he was dead. Suddenly my mind went so blank that I never thought to feel for a pulse—or listen to his heart. "Julian," I whispered a little louder, a little more frantically, reaching out to shake him, knowing his eyes were open, thinking he must be hearing me—"Julian, wake up!"

It was at that moment the flute stopped.

It was at that moment I realized he should have been breathing very heavily—gasping, even heaving, struggling much more than I was for a lungful of air.

After the way he had fought me for the angel dust and swirled around the garden, then collapsed with such violence against the bricks, he should have been . . .

He should have been . . .

"Julian," I whispered again, this time in my mind, remembering some words I had once read, remembering some death I had once feared, holding my breath and putting my ear to his chest and finally hearing a beat so far, so faint that I thought . . . I knew that Julian must be . . . screaming for me . . .

Screaming inside for me . . .

Unable to get it out for me . . .

My God, Julian.

Oh my God, Julian . . .

I am heartily sorry, Julian . . .

For having offended . . .

For having intended . . .

"Julian!" I cried out, suddenly waving my arms, suddenly pounding his chest, unable to take my eyes off his eyes . . .

Unable to turn my head or pull away from him . . .

Just staring as if down some street I had followed him to—or some window I was watching him through—until finally . . .

Finally I did the only thing that made any real sense—that would at least give me a chance of surviving (of not having to live with his death as I had with his life)—I . . .

I reached out very slowly and closed both his eyes, as if closing blinds.

I remember saying a prayer and seeing one tear as I confined his death, as if sex, to the darkness. . . .